D0897920

226

Williamston High School
Williamston, Michigan

THE ENEMY

Bombs began to fall on the Hawaiian Islands at 7:55 in the morning. It was Sunday, December 7, 1941.

The enemy had given no warning to, nor had made any declaration of war against, the United States of America. His dive-bombing and torpedo planes swirled down from a peaceful sky in a sneak attack which is known now as "A Day of Infamy."

The bombs and torpedoes of the enemy sank five of the eight United States Navy's battleships moored in Hawaii's Pearl Harbor. They severely damaged a sixth battleship, and of the last two both were hard-hit. His attack also sank two destroyers and nine other ships and ruined over 150 aircraft.

The enemy killed that morning more than three thousand citizens of the United States.

Of the three U. S. Navy aircraft carriers then in the Pacific, the enemy hit none, for by chance the carriers were not in Pearl Harbor that day.

John Lawrence, a young naval aviator aboard the aircraft carrier *Enterprise*, heard the news of the attack with the same stunned surprise and instant outrage that the news caused all over the world.

Until that day in December, John Lawrence had never

stopped to think that his country would actually ask him to give his life to protect it. During his days as an aviation cadet in flight training at Pensacola, Florida, he had not seriously considered that he was being trained to fight an enemy of his country. Wars were raging—in China, in Europe, in Great Britain. But there was no war at Pensacola; just the long hot days grinding the old N3N biplanes above the flat Florida coast land and the long hot nights in the dull-red brick barracks.

War to him had been remote; he did not know an enemy. His concern was to learn to fly an airplane, and this had taken about all the time for thought he had.

He did not know it that Sunday afternoon as he and his brother Jeff walked on the flight deck of the *Enterprise*, but on the starboard side of his ship, a ship was steaming which would soon be sunk. A doomed ship sailed on his port side, also.

Even with the terrible news from Pearl Harbor still pouring in, the war to John Lawrence still seemed unreal, impossible.

He wondered what he would do when at last he, himself, would be caught up in the actual combat. He wondered if he would be brave or be a coward.

(John Lawrence would not have felt so lonely and afraid if he had known that every man aboard the *Enterprise* was at that moment wondering exactly the same thing.)

John could not even talk to his older brother Jeff about these secret doubts. He would have to wait and sweat out the answer; wait until June of 1942.

And while he waited the enemy swept on, capturing the Philippines, Malaya, the Netherlands East Indies; burning, pillaging, destroying as he advanced across the Pacific.

The enemy was never defeated; his assaults on the Pacific

islands were never stopped, or even blunted, in those months following his monstrous victory over the United States Navy at Pearl Harbor.

But then June of 1942 came for the enemy . . . and for John Lawrence.

PART ONE

COMBAT

1

John Lawrence had the vague feeling that something was wrong. Looking down and to his left, he could see the aircraft carrier *Enterprise* plowing straight ahead, her flight deck crowded with planes forward but clear aft for his landing. He could see the plane handlers in their bright-colored uniforms waiting for him; see the Landing Signal officer standing there with his flags looking up at him.

John looked down into the cockpit. His altitude was about right; air speed okay, everything okay. But there was still that vague feeling that something was wrong. Maybe not right now, but in a minute something was going to foul up; he was going to goof.

Somehow, John thought as he banked for the approach, more things went wrong for him than for other people. For instance, the first plane he had cracked up. The N3N biplane during flight training at Pensacola. That one had almost washed him out of naval aviation, but it hadn't been his fault at all. The board of inquiry had put it down as ninety per cent pilot error but they had been wrong. His landing had been all right—perhaps a little fast and a little far down the runway, but all right. Only there was no point in letting the plane roll forever; it just meant taxiing back a mile or so—getting in the way, holding up traffic. So he had applied the normal amount of brakes.

There must have been something wrong with the brakes. As soon as he pressed down on them, he felt the smooth rolling of the plane jerk to a stop. For an instant he just sat there, the motor running, the propeller a silver disc in front of him, and then the plane nosed up. When the whirling prop tips hit the concrete runway they splintered, filling the air with slivers of wood. The engine jammed to a sudden stop, and for a long, teetering moment the airplane stood straight up on its nose. John remembered hoping hard that it would settle back on its wheels but it did not. It went on over on its back, and there he was hanging upside down, held there by his seat belt, his head only inches from the concrete.

If the thing had caught on fire it would have been by-by Aviation Cadet John Lawrence, USNR, but it didn't burn. It just lay there on its back, and for a long time there was silence until the whine and roar and clang of the fire truck and ambulance started up as they tore down the runway.

John felt like a fool hanging there helpless, upside down, and the remark of the ensign who got him loose didn't help any. "Intrepid birdman," the ensign said as John, free of the belt, fell out of the plane onto the hard runway.

That was the first one—the first plane, anyway. There had been worse ones. . . .

It was time now for the final approach to the flight deck. Wheels—down. Flaps—down. Tail hook—down.

In the turn he lost a little altitude so gunned her to get it back. Now he was straight behind the carrier, a mile or so aft of it, and everything seemed all right.

Maybe, John thought, this vague feeling of coming disaster

was only because he was tired. He had been flying a long and weary search out over the empty sea; the weather had been foul, the horizon broken by enormous thunderstorms like black castles which had thrown the plane violently, forcing him to fight it all the way.

John glanced down at the Pacific. It had changed from the blue of daylight to the black of night which to John was far more menacing and dangerous.

He took a quick look behind to make sure no one was crowding him, although he knew that he was the last plane in the air.

Night fell so *fast* our here, he thought. In the States a night could take hours to fall, but out here in the western Pacific it changed from day to night in only a few minutes. The sun went down and—*wham*—it was dark.

It was dark now; the shape of the carrier was blending into the color of the black sea as John gunned her a little more and held her straight and level. As he came closer, the way the deck looked began to change. From a mile back the deck looked as though it were a fine, level runway—as easy to land on as an airport in Kansas. But as you came closer, you began to see the true movement of the deck. If the waves weren't too rough it wasn't so bad, but now huge waves were running and the deck ahead looked like an express elevator rushing up and down. It was also slithering from side to side and at the same time, rocking like a wild chair.

These were the seconds John always hated—these last fumbling seconds of flying the plane toward the stern of the ship; seconds when you were no longer absolute master of the plane but had to give up some control of it to the Landing Signal officer with the little flags who stood on the flight deck and took over the flying for you.

These were moments he had a right to hate, John thought.

You were breaking all the rules now by flying low and slow,
the plane barely under control. Mistakes now were deadly,
and there never seemed time enough to correct them once
you made them.

Looking ahead, he watched the Landing Signal officer. Lt.
(j.g.) Conklin was about as unmilitary as you could get without trying. He was a round, plump, pink man, about the
minimum height to get in the Navy, with bowlegs and flappy
ears. Everything not covered by his uniform (and he made a
uniform look like rumpled pajamas) was red. His hair was
red, his face and hands were eternally red, not brown, from
the sun, and the effort of looking into the sky at planes all
day gave even his eyes a reddish tint. He was forever sunburned and forever slathered in one sort of ointment or another in his useless efforts to stop being sunburned. That was
his only complaint. "With a complexion like mine," Conklin
would cry, "the Navy should have stationed me in the Arctic
where there are six months of darkness. So here I am in the
middle of the sunny Pacific being turned into a lobster."

They said he was the best LSO in the Navy. He had been
a naval aviator, and a good one, but he had turned in his
wings just before Pearl Harbor. His reason for doing that
would have made John feel ashamed, but it didn't seem to
bother Conklin. "I got scared," Conklin would tell you.
"That's all. And who wants to fly wingman on a scared
pilot?"

Conklin now had the two flags in his hands and was
signaling to John that he was too low and drifting to the left.
John gunned her up and pulled her straight again. Conklin
held the flags steady and John relaxed a little.

It was a funny thing, he thought, watching Conklin. One
minute you were a pilot, flying your plane. It was up to you
to make your own decisions—*you* decided to go up or down

or slow or fast, to roll her or loop her, dive her or fly her on her back. It was up to you and nobody else. Then, as you came toward the carrier, those flags took over. Those two little bright-colored flags in Conklin's hands suddenly took away from you all decision. Those little flags could save your life—they had saved John's once or twice. They could kill you, too.

2

Lt. (j.g.) Raymond Conklin stood at the very end of the flight deck and watched the SBD Dauntless coming in for a landing. It was the last plane of the search flight, the last *Enterprise* plane in the air. Get this one aboard, Conklin thought, and this day will be over. He had been out on the deck since dawn, the sun merciless on him, as the routine flights of Combat Air Patrol and Anti-Submarine Patrol planes had been launched or taken aboard. In addition, planes had been searching all day, for it was rumored the enemy was on the move again.

As the plane approached, Conklin forgot that he was hungry and tired and hurting as he concentrated on the flight. He knew by the way the plane was handled that it was John Lawrence, just as he knew how every pilot aboard handled his plane. Conklin wished that it was John's brother Jeff. But it wasn't—so get him aboard.

Conklin stood on the starboard side of the flight deck, to the left of incoming pilots, and held, one in each hand, small red-and-yellow-striped flags. To a pilot he was an airplane—the pilot's airplane. Conklin's body was the fuselage, his arms and the flags were the wings. If a pilot's left wing was down, Conklin's right arm with its flag would go down. If a pilot was too high, Conklin would make a "down" motion with the flags. When at last Conklin had maneuvered the plane into an attitude where it could be flown safely on board he would stand, the flags out straight and level, until, when he was sure a landing could be made, he would slash a flag across his throat with a swift gesture. This was the "Cut." At this instant the pilot turned off his engine and landed.

However, in this same last moment if Conklin decided that the plane was too fast or too slow or high or low, or the arresting hook in the tail of the plane wasn't down—or for any other reason that he thought might ruin the landing—he would wave the flags in a gesture of command. This—the "Wave-Off"—meant to the pilot to shove his throttle open, pull up, get out and go around again.

Just behind Conklin was a small canvas screen which did two things. It kept the blast of the thirty or more knots of wind from hammering him all day, and it provided a clear background against which the pilots could see exactly what he was doing with the flags.

To Conklin's right there was the edge of the flight deck and five feet below the emergency net and the catwalk. This narrow walkway ran the full length of the flight deck and made it possible for men to move around without getting up on the deck and in the way of planes landing or taking off. Guns to protect the ship were also mounted on the catwalk. For Conklin the catwalk was a place of escape in case of trouble. If, as happened too often, an unexpectedly big wave lifted the stern of the *Enterprise* up into the path of a landing plane, there wasn't much a pilot could do. His plane was by then going so slow that pulling up was almost impossible as in front of him the steel stern of the ship suddenly loomed up as a solid barrier.

When planes struck the stern head on, Conklin would dive into the emergency net. As soon as he was down below the level of the flight deck, he would raise his head cautiously until his eyes were again above the deck. Most of the time the planes which struck the stern would simply drop off and into the sea, but sometimes they would strike at such an attitude that they would hang there, demolished. Then there would be aviation gasoline all over everything and in seconds the explosive fire. Conklin then could either run away or try to help. Sometimes when he thought he could save a pilot he would help. When he didn't think he could, he ran.

When things went right, which was most of the time, Conklin would give the pilot his cut and as the plane swept past him, Conklin would step out from behind his little screen and watch the rest of the landing. By this time, of course, the flight deck crew would have put the wires up so that to Conklin (who wasn't very tall) it looked as though there were almost two decks—the solid one and the one made of heavy stranded wires which were stretched tight a foot or so above the deck and ran from side to side of it. These wires were held by heavy hydraulic springs which, when the arresting hook hanging from the tail of the plane caught a wire, brought the plane to a halt. Then the wires would be lowered back into their slots in the deck, and the plane would taxi on forward and be parked beyond the barrier.

The barrier was a strong fence also made of wire, but it had many strands of very heavy cable which, if a plane out of control struck them, would give a little but were supposed to stop it before it could ram into the parked planes in the bow of the ship.

Now John Lawrence was bringing the Dauntless in. Conklin always worried about John. It wasn't that John was a poor pilot, nor even that he was a mediocre pilot—he could be very good. Maybe, Conklin thought now, it's just that John wasn't as lucky as, say, his brother Jeff. Or, Conklin wondered, perhaps John hasn't got that burning drive to fly that some men have so that when things went wrong, John accepted them instead of fighting them the way some men did.

So Conklin always worried a little about John's landings and he was worrying now, although the plane was coming in very nicely, straight on, speed just right, high enough to clear the stern, low enough not to go beyond the third wire.

Behind the plane now the sky was black. The thunderstorm which had been making up all afternoon had now broken some miles behind the *Enterprise,* and there was a solid wall of black rain rising from the sea to the black clouds.

Conklin thought afterwards that the blackness of the sky behind the plane had been the real cause of what happened and he had tried to convince the skipper that it had been his fault and not John's, but the fact remained that the tail hook of John's plane was either not down all the way or as some witnesses claimed, not down at all.

At any rate, as John's plane came toward Conklin in the last seconds of its flight, everything seemed fine. It was only in the last second that Conklin saw the trouble. In fact, Conklin had already started the movement of the flag toward his throat for the cut and had to jerk his arm back and give John a frantic wave-off.

John saw the little flags, colors dimmed by darkness, start the cut and then grow wild in the wave-off. All the motions for taking the cut had to be instantly stopped. Instead of pulling the throttle back he now jammed it forward—all the way. In a single instant he had to take the airplane away from Conklin and the flags; he had to fly it again.

There simply was not time and space enough to save it. The airplane, engine and prop screaming, wheels coming up, nose rising, clawed for its life. . . .

3

On the bridge of the carrier, the captain and John's brother Jeff were standing behind the splinter shield watching the plane coming in for its landing. In a moment, the captain knew, every nerve in his body would go slack. It was a peculiar feeling—as though for a second all his strength was gone. It was, he knew, only the reaction of deep relief when the last plane got aboard.

For the captain of a carrier, take-offs and landings out here in the western Pacific were times of great trial. A captain knew, of course, that he had put his ship where it was for the sole purpose of flying airplanes off it and taking them back aboard again. Without the planes the carrier had no reason to exist. But at the same time, with enemy submarines everywhere and enemy planes in the stormy sky, to put his ship on a straight course and hold her there for as long as it took the planes to take off from her deck and—always—the longer time to get them back aboard was—*each time*—an invitation for the enemy to come and kill the ship.

But now the last plane of the search was coming aboard. The approach looked good, even though the captain and John's brother Jeff were now above the level of the plane.

At least, the captain thought, if the weather is so bad that we can't fly, neither can the enemy. In a few seconds now he would be able to turn and say, "Resume base course; resume zigzag pattern able." In a few seconds the feeling of waiting for disaster would be over. Waiting for the unseen torpedo to strike, the whistling bomb to drop, the shell from nowhere to plunge into his ship, would be ended.

As the captain watched the plane coming in, he felt again a dread of decision which always plagued him. In the peacetime Navy, if a man went overboard everything possible was done to save him. Ships stopped dead in the water, lifeboats were lowered, hours and days would be spent searching the sea for the one man lost in it. But not in war. If a man went overboard now no ships stopped, no boats were lowered, no search was made. Not even a life ring was dropped, for it would leave a telltale sign for the enemy.

This thing plagued the captain. He could reason all he wanted to that to stop a ship for one man was risking the ship and all its thousands of men, but he could not forget the sight of one man lost overboard, swimming desperately toward the retreating ship until at last he had to give up, and the captain saw him for the last time, waving one arm above the water in a gesture of fatal farewell.

As the captain watched John's plane in its final moments of landing, he put the thought of a man overboard out of his mind by remembering the slip of paper in his pocket. Without saying anything he got it out and handed it to Jeff.

Jeff took the piece of paper and read it swiftly for his attention was on his brother's landing.

The paper said: Large enemy force with all types of combatant ships approaching Midway.

The captain said, "What do you make of that, Commander?"

"Bound to be a scuffle," Jeff said.

"A scuffle," the captain said, vaguely.

Jeff handed the piece of paper back. He could not now really concentrate on the information for he was physically flying his brother's plane in for its landing. He was in the cockpit—now turning off the ignition, now holding her steady, feeling her dropping out from under him toward the deck only a few inches below. Now he was bracing himself for that moment when the tail hook caught the wire. There was nothing in the world, he thought, quite like that feeling. At one moment you and the plane were air-borne, flying, softly and almost silently. In the next moment all motion was slammed out of the plane and you were sitting there, motionless. He wondered if other pilots had the same reaction he did. For an instant, somehow you felt like a fool.

He waited as John's plane settled, waited for the roar of the engine to stop, waited for the hard thump of the wheels and the creaking cry of the wire against the springs.

Instead the engine's noise changed into a deep scream; the plane began to stagger upward, the sound of the propeller changing as the pitch was changed.

Jeff pulled the plane upward with every muscle and bone he had.

It wasn't enough.

4

For a moment John thought that he was going to make it. As the plane roared forward only inches above the flight deck it gained, inch by inch, a little altitude. Slowly—so slowly—the sluggishness of its flight was changing into real flight, control was coming back into the stick in John's hand and the pedals against his feet.

Ahead of him the cables of the barrier looked black and oily. Beyond the cables the entire forward end of the deck was crowded with planes, their wings folded up against the black sky. The men who had been working among these planes now suddenly stopped and turned and stared. John, on a level with them, could see their faces like white marks in the darkness.

He didn't want to hit the barrier. He had seen planes do that.

The barrier could stop a plane which had torn loose from a wire or a plane skidding in wheels up, but it couldn't stop a plane in free flight coming in as fast as he was. Nothing but a solid wall could stop him now. If he hit the barrier he would flip over it, as he had seen others do, and go upside down, crashing into the planes parked beyond it.

There was always fire then, and unless the crew moved very fast, the fire would explode whatever bombs or torpedoes were in the parked planes.

It wasn't often a pilot came out of that one alive.

John held the SBD nose high at the very point of stalling and felt the plane rising.

And then a ninth wave struck the bow of the *Enterprise* and flowed down along her sides, lifting her up and up.

It was as though the wave had reached up into the sky and dragged the airplane down.

As the rising deck slammed up against the plane, John felt the old, terrible emptiness of failure. Somehow, to him it also had a taste—dry and bitter.

The impact of the rising deck and the lift of the plane threw it back into the air, but it was no longer in flight.

John stared at the barrier and the dark planes beyond it and the men now scurrying for safety. It seemed to him then that he said out loud, "I don't want to burn to death," but if he did no one heard him above the roar of the engine, the clanging of the alarm gongs, the yelling of men and the howling of the wind over the deck.

He had a few feet of altitude now as the wave passed under and dropped the ship into the trough, and he had a little forward speed remaining.

He rammed the left rudder pedal to the floor, slammed the stick hard to the left and with his body tried to force the plane to turn away from the looming barrier and, if possible, to clear the ship, although he knew that he and his plane were doomed.

Time and distance ran out for him then. The plane tilted hard to the left, screaming as it turned, but the left wing tip struck the flight deck and crumpled. For a moment, to those watching, the plane seemed to stand there on its broken wing. But then it fell, cartwheeling, the engine screaming.

The propeller blades striking the deck put a brutal stop to the engine and let the plane go on cartwheeling, but now in silence.

It destroyed itself across the deck and then fell from the ship.

The last thing John saw clearly was a man's face—a gunner in the port catwalk—staring up at him. The man's eyes were strangely filled with compassion, John thought, as he looked into them. Death had missed the man by inches, and yet he stood there, fearful only for John's own death as the plane began the long drop to the black and stormy sea.

5

As the captain watched John's plane hurtling toward the barrier, ice and sickness formed in his stomach and rage actually burned in his mind. Not rage at John personally, but rage that in a moment, through carelessness, bad flying, he would lose his ship. It would be blown apart, and the thousands of gallons of gas and oil in it, the bombs and torpedoes and ammunition would rip and burn it until it sank.

But then miraculously, he saw the plane turning. You couldn't call it flight—it was more as though a fitful wind was blowing the thing.

The captain leaned far forward watching, his whole body urging the plane to rise and turn and *fly*, to become again an aircraft lifted by its wings and moved by its propeller, to regain the sky. To go away.

Jeff, beside the captain, also leaned forward trying to push his strength and skill and knowledge out from the carrier's island, out across the flight deck to his brother.

"That's my brother," Jeff said.

"I know," the captain said.

The plane's left wing tip struck the flight deck and the wing was torn away at the root. The blow cartwheeled the plane and the whirling propeller struck.

"Good," Jeff said aloud, as he saw that John had cut the ignition in time. Now at least, he thought, it may not catch on fire.

Now the plane stood almost straight up on its nose on the port edge of the flight deck. Men in the port catwalk ran for their lives as the murderous plane hovered above them. It looked helpless and a little ridiculous balanced there, one wing torn off, the propeller a twisted tripod under it. Then it slowly fell and disappeared below the level of the deck.

Jeff turned, hoping but knowing it was useless, to gaze at the captain.

The captain turned his head a little and said, "Man overboard." He said it automatically, as in the years past he had been taught to do. He said it sadly, because he knew that the ship would not hesitate so much as one beat of the propellers.

Then the captain turned and looked at Jeff, the sadness in his eyes.

Jeff turned fast and ran down the ladder of the island and out onto the flight deck. He ran aft to the very edge of the deck and there with the LSO, Conklin, he stood leaning over, peering down.

6

It was a long, long way to fall. And so quiet. John was surprised by how long it took for the plane and him to fall all that way, and by how quiet it was. The plane itself made no sound at all so that John could hear the sound of the sea through which the ship moved; he could occasionally hear his plane strike and slide a little way against the steel hull of the ship; and all the time, he could hear the throb and pound of the ship's engines and motors, breathing, and a heart beat.

He was so close to the side of the carrier that it gave him the feeling that he was not falling but that the gray side of the ship was rising.

Then he struck the water. He hit much harder than he had expected, and in an instant the motion of falling was changed into a motion of being swept away, the gray hull rushing in a different direction.

For a moment he just sat there in the ruined and sinking plane and stared stupidly at the ship. Waves striking the hull threw heavy salt spray into his face, burning his eyes, wetting his clothing. This annoyed him. Didn't he have enough trouble already without that?

They won't stop, he thought. Not for me.

He scrubbed the salt water out of his eyes and looked again. The ship now seemed far away, almost lost, its gray-

ness blending fast into the dark gray of the stormy sky, the
gray and black of the sea.

Water, solid water, rising in his lap caught his attention,
and for a second he stared at it. Then, oddly without haste
or fumbling, he reached down into the water and opened
the buckle of the safety belt. Next he unloosed the harness
around his shoulders and shrugged out of the straps of the
parachute. Then as he started to stand up in the cockpit, he
remembered that it was his duty to destroy the secret
electronic gear in the plane and to be sure that all charts
and codes and other papers which could aid the enemy were
wrapped with weights so that they would sink to the bottom
of the sea.

When he turned the switch which was supposed to blow
up the electronic gear, nothing happened. Probably too soaked
with water, he thought. But it didn't matter. The sea was
deep here, miles deep, and everything was going down with
the plane.

Charts and codes he stuffed into a canvas bag, weighted
with lead, and dropped into the water. It sank into the darkness, and he wondered for a second how long it would take
it to reach that dark bottom where for a million years nothing
had disturbed the ooze or slime or whatever it was down
there.

Then, just as he was about to leave the plane, he remembered being warned: never leave anything floating on the
surface, because to a trailing submarine it would say that a
ship had passed this way.

Never leave anything floating on the surface, he thought,
as he half climbed, half floated out of the sinking cockpit.

Only me.

As the plane at last, with much bubbling and hissing, went

completely under, he pulled the lanyards of the CO_2 bottles stuck into the waistband of the yellow Mae West life jacket, and they added their hiss and bubbling to that of the plane as they inflated the awkward vest.

The water was warm enough, and floating softly in the Mae West, the stormy waves didn't bother him as he rode them up and down, up and down. On the crests he would look for his ship but the sky was dark and stormy, the sea disturbed under the wind, and he could not make her out. He knew, as all the pilots well knew, that the carrier would not turn and come back and stop to save his life.

It was lonely here. The loneliest place he had even been.

7

The skipper of the plane guard destroyer following in the wake of the *Enterprise* said, "Rig out a bosun's chair, starboard side."

The sailor at the P.A. system repeated, "Rig bosun's chair starboard side."

The skipper of the destroyer leaned to a voice tube and said, "Look alert up there." And a faint, mechanical voice answered, "Alert, aye, aye, sir."

"What do you see?" the skipper asked.

"Nothing, Captain."

The destroyer struck a wave bow on which threw her back on her screws and drowned her from forepeak to the top of the bridge.

"And they call this Pacific," the skipper said, rubbing his arm where he had bruised it against the bulkhead.

"Chair manned and ready," a sailor said and the skipper nodded.

The skipper said, "Tell the engine room to stand by for some pretty violent maneuvers."

A solid wall of rain now struck the ship and streamed down the glass ports of the bridge. The rain, though, calmed the sea a little so that the skipper no longer had to brace himself in the doorway.

He made his way over to stand beside the helmsman. "Didn't you drive a taxi before you got greeted?" he asked the helmsman.

The helmsman, too busy fighting the wheel to talk, only nodded.

"Well, I want some of that fancy taxi driving now."

"Yes, sir," the helmsman said. "But in weather like this I'd park the heap and go get a beer, sir."

The skipper looked at him not unpleasantly. "Look at it this way," the skipper said. "You're the one out there in the water all by yourself."

8

It was the loneliest place John had ever been. As a great wave lifted him up, he looked all around the close horizon. His carrier had now vanished entirely, and all he could see was sky the color of old lead, water the color of deep evening, and behind him, solid rain.

In a moment the rain began to fall on him.

That was too much. The rain was cold as ice and came down hard, stinging his face. As he began to cry he was suddenly ashamed and embarrassed, but he went on crying.

What else, he asked himself, is there to do?

9

The skipper of the destroyer ordered, "Have four men and the pharmacist's mate stand by, starboard side. Get some blankets up there, too. And a stretcher."

The executive officer of the can who had come into the bridge asked, "Do you think you're going to find anything, Skipper?"

Before the skipper answered he asked the soundman, "What do you hear, Sound?"

"Nothing, sir. The rain is drowning out everything."

"Sub could be aiming a shot at us two feet away," the exec said.

The skipper nodded. "That's why I don't want to have to make but one pass. If we—find anything."

"Will you stop her dead in the water?" the exec asked.

These two men were friends and sailors, they understood each other very well. The skipper looked at the exec for a moment and then nodded.

The exec turned away and looked out into the rain. The war is so big, he thought. So *huge*, covering oceans and continents, with whole nations involved. But was war, he wondered, ever bigger than life? Even one man's life?

10

John had stopped crying and lay in the water, listening because there was nothing else to do. He couldn't hear a thing except the almost tinny sound of the rain striking the sea and below that, the sound of the sea itself—a dull, steady sound.

Because he was shielding his face from the lash of the rain, he didn't see it. And because of the sound of rain and sea, he didn't hear it.

One moment he was lost and dying in the Pacific. Next moment a steel boat hook caught him by the belt and jerked him upward, dripping and helpless, and banged him hard against the steel hull of the destroyer. Hands now reached down through the rain and grabbed him wherever they could find a grip. They scraped him up the rough side and tumbled him over the steel lifelines and put him gently down on the streaming deck.

A voice said, "All ahead standard, course two one zero," and another voice, coming from a face close over him, "You hurt?"

John shook his head. "I'm okay. Just wet."

"Take him to sick bay. Let me know." The skipper of the destroyer went fast up the ladder to the bridge and closed the door behind him.

When they tried to put John on the stretcher, he pushed them away and stood up. "I'm okay," he told them. "Just wet."

11

The ride back to the *Enterprise* in the breeches buoy was almost as rough on John as the fall from the deck. Hanging in the ridiculous canvas breeches, his legs dangling through the holes, he was hauled across from the destroyer to the high deck of the carrier. As waves flung the ships closer together or farther apart, the motion either dunked John into the sizzling water or jerked him like a puppet on a string far into the air, only to stop him with a bone-jarring slam against the cables. He wondered halfway across why they were going to so much trouble for just one pilot?

He found out.

His brother Jeff was there on the *Enterprise*'s dark deck to greet him, standing in the falling rain. As John got painfully to his feet, he said, "Goofed again."

"Goofed?" Jeff asked. "If you hadn't turned it when you did we'd all be in the water. How do you feel?"

"Stupid," John said.

"You'd better check into sick bay and let the docs look you over. Then I'll see you in the ready room. Big doings," Jeff said.

They went together to the light baffle leading into the island of the carrier. John opened the outer door and they stepped into a small compartment. When John shut the door it was totally dark in there until he opened the inner door to the ship. Now there was faint and eerie blue light around them.

And the awful smell of the ship struck them.

John had always hated this night smell of the carrier. At sunset every night all openings leading to the outside were closed so that no light would show the lurking enemy where the ship was on the dark sea. This closing up of the ship shut up inside it all the heat and smells and foul odors— smells of hot oil from the engines, of ozone from sparking brushes, smells of long-unwashed men, and of smoke and paint and garbage and refuse, of bad breath from two thousand mouths. By dawn when the ship could be opened again to the fresh air of the Pacific, you could cut the foul air inside the ship with a knife and carry it on a plate.

But tonight John loved the foul odors and the awful heat which could make your sweat come dripping through the bottom of your mattress as you slept. He loved the dim blue light and the low pipes on which he bumped his head, the bare steel and the neglected paint of a fighting ship. This, he thought, is home.

The doctors in sick bay found nothing wrong with him and in a little while let him go—to return at last as a pilot; not a lucky one, but a live one.

John made his way up through the dim blue light to the pilot's ready room just under the flight deck. From this room with its comfortable chairs, the pilots could run out onto the catwalk and thus on up to the deck with its waiting planes. This ready room was almost more a home for the pilots than the rooms they slept in, for in the ready room the air was clean and conditioned, the chairs were soft and good for sleeping. There were always men in here to talk with, or just to sit with and fight back the loneliness of knowing that tomorrow or the next day, you or the man next to you might be dead.

The ready room was very quiet when he got there. A few of the pilots were playing cards, a few were sleeping in the reclining chairs, a few reading, a few writing. To John it looked just as it always looked when nothing much was going on. But it didn't feel the same. There was something different about it, he thought, as he found an empty chair and slumped down into it, still aching and bruised from the fall and the breeches buoy. Something was different—a tension in here, an apprehension, a fear perhaps.

And then he looked up at the blackboard which covered almost one wall of the room. Someone had written in chalk:

AN ATTACK BY THE ENEMY FOR THE PUR-
POSE OF CAPTURING MIDWAY ISLAND IS EX-
PECTED. THE ATTACKING FORCE MAY BE COM-
POSED OF ALL COMBATANT TYPES INCLUDING
FOUR OR FIVE BIG CARRIERS.

John was staring at this when his brother Jeff came in and sat down beside him.

"Going to be a short night," Jeff said, waving at the blackboard. "We sighted them this afternoon. Troop transports and seaplane tenders about seven hundred miles from Midway. Sailing eastward at about nineteen knots."

"Then there's going to be a fight?" John asked.

"Wouldn't be surprised."

"What do they want with Midway? That's about as nothing an island as I ever heard of."

"They don't want Midway, they want us."

As John turned to look at him, the door to the ready room opened and the Air Combat Intelligence officer came in. This man was older than all of them, a lean, sick-looking man with large horn-rimmed glasses and thinning hair. He looked exactly like what he had been before the war—a banker in New York. But now he was a lieutenant in the Navy with the job of telling the pilots what to expect when they took off from their ship and went out over the lonely or crowded ocean.

"All right," the ACI officer said, "All hands wake up and pay attention."

The pilots put away their cards and books and letters, the sleeping were nudged awake, and when they were all alert and listening the ACI officer said: "Just remember this: the Japs haven't lost a battle yet. They whipped us at Pearl Harbor and knocked out every battleship we had. They whipped the British. They have conquered the Philippines and Java and the East Indies. And last month they whipped us again in the Battle of the Coral Sea and sunk the *Lexington* to boot."

The pilots all turned and looked at one man. A thin, pale-faced pilot who had never smiled since he had come aboard.

His name was Simpson but they all thought of him as "The Survivor." He had been a pilot on the *Lexington* when she went down and he had not forgotten it.

The ACI officer went on: "The enemy's plan is very simple and so far it has worked very well. He rules the Pacific from Australia all the way up to where we are right now. He wants to rule the rest of it. He wants to move up on through the Aleutians, taking Midway, the Hawaiian Islands, Samoa and Fiji, and all the rest as he goes."

John asked again, "What does he want with Midway?"

"I'm getting to that," the ACI officer told him. "If the enemy can master the whole Pacific, then he rules everything from Asia to the western coast of the United States itself. With our eastern shores threatened by Germany and our western shores lost to Japan, we must eventually go down under the weight of all the rest of the world against us."

There was absolute silence in the ready room so that the throb and hum and pound of the ship sounded loud and close around them.

"So to answer your question, John," the ACI officer went on, "I'll ask another one. What is the only thing that can break up this plan of his? What is the only thing that can stop him from taking the whole Pacific?"

The thin man stopped and looked at them for a moment. "Us," he said. "Only us."

There was silence again as each of the pilots lounging in the chairs thought his own thoughts. The war was enormous; the plans of nations to conquer oceans and continents were enormous. But these pilots were thinking: there's going to be a fight tomorrow, and I'll have to fly well and shoot well and be lucky or I'll never sit in this chair again.

The ACI officer went on. "He'll take Midway—or try to— because it's a nuisance to him. From Midway our patrol planes can hunt him out in his own backyard. They can't hurt him but they can tell us where he is and what he's doing. Midway is a splinter in his thumb and he would like to pull it out.

"But taking Midway isn't the big thing now. The big thing is—us. The U. S. Pacific Fleet—which is us—is more than a splinter in his thumb. It's a gun pointing at him. Not a big gun, but a gun, and before he can go any further, he's got to get rid of us. He thinks he can. And he has no reason not to. He's whipped us every time he's tackled us so that now we are weaker than we have ever been—and he is stronger. That's why he's launching this attack on a miserable little sandy island out here in the middle of nowhere. An island only the gooney birds like."

The ACI officer turned to the blackboard.

"We don't *know*," he said, "we can only guess, but Admiral Nimitz is guessing that this attack on Midway is a feint. They want what's left of the U. S. Navy to come out and fight so that they can whip us again and this time destroy us completely, so that they can go on with their plan to conquer the Pacific and sail their ships to the Golden Gate at San Francisco. Well, we've come out to meet them, and I think we're ready to fight."

He wrote on the blackboard:

US   THEM

"With the *Lexington* at the bottom of the sea, bless her heart, we've only got three carriers left to fight with: The *Yorktown,* and *Enterprise* and *Hornet*."

He wrote 3 carriers under US.

"They will have five carriers, at least."

Under THEM he wrote 5 carriers.

"We have no battleships at all."

Some pilot in the back row said, "Good!" and they all laughed.

The ACI officer said, "If it comes down to a slugging match, we'll wish we had a few because they'll have a dozen or more."

Under US he wrote BB zero. Under THEM he wrote BB 12 plus.

"In cruisers we're about even—around eight apiece."

He wrote 8 under US and THEM.

"He will swamp us with destroyers. Maybe fifty. We have fifteen."

He wrote 15 and 50 under US and THEM.

"Since some of you think that the entire Navy exists only so you can fly around up there in the Air Corps' wild blue yonder, let's see how we stand in planes."

A few of the pilots smiled at this but not many and not for long, for to them this was the heart and soul of the fight.

"It isn't good," the ACI officer told them. "We have a total of 220 planes aboard the three carriers. Let's say two hundred will be fit to fly. The enemy is going to slam at least three hundred planes against you with three hundred pilots who have fought before."

He wrote 200 under US and 300 under THEM and then he turned around and quietly said, "So let's go out and beat them."

No one said anything.

"We should find them in the morning," he said. "Hit the carriers. Let everything else go and get those carriers. All right, here are the details."

There was a movement and rustling in the ready room while the pilots got out their chart boards and took notes, as the ACI officer wrote the details of enemy strength and course and speed and disposition.

The ACI officer was only estimating the enemy's strength and guessing at his position, for he had not yet heard that the Battle for Midway had already started.

12

At about four-thirty that afternoon, nine Army Air Corps B-17's which had taken off from Midway Island spotted the enemy's attack transports now 570 miles from Midway. These planes made a high-level bombing run, but although they claimed to have hit two battleships, actually all their bombs fell harmlessly into the Pacific.

Following the B-17's, four of the Navy's lumbering old flying boats, Catalinas, each armed with one torpedo, made a run on the enemy's troop transports but they, too, had very little luck and only hit one oiler—and that only hard enough to kill twenty-three men and to slow it down for a little while.

And so, at midnight, June 4, 1942, began.

13

In the cabin where John lived with three other pilots, there was now only the dim blue glow of the battlelight. There were four bunks here, attached to the bulkheads, two on each side of the room, one above the other. John's was the top bunk, starboard side, and he had learned the hard way never to sit up in it, for the steel housing of the catapult sheave was only inches above it and could split your skull if you weren't careful.

The air in the cabin was hot and foul, and the fan whirring

monotonously did nothing but move the stuff slowly around the room.

John, who had not been able to sleep at all, was now almost hating the other three men in the room. For they slept. Not easily, nor deeply, but they slept. John lay in the blue light looking over and down at them and in a detached way hated each one of them. Strickland, in the lower bunk, lay naked and uncovered, the blue light glowing on the sweat forming and running off his body while the moving band of air from the oscillating fan waved the hairs on his chest back and forth. Strickland slept and snored and sweated. Directly below John, Hendricks moved in his sleep trying to find a cool spot in the hot, sweat-wet bed but never finding it. Across the room from John, Simpson, The Survivor of the *Lexington*, moaned in his sleep, a pitiful and frightening sound.

John lay there hoping that the nausea which was working in his stomach and sending gushes of cold spit around his teeth was only the result of the salt water he had swallowed —and not fear. But as the nausea grew and took command of him, he knew that it wasn't salt water.

He tried his best to defeat it—he forced his clenched fingers to open and relax, he forced his mind to stop thinking about what might happen in the morning, he tried to lie there limp and vacant, he tried to close his eyes and sleep.

When he opened them after only a moment, The Survivor was no longer in his bunk.

John thought: he, too, must vomit. It made him feel a little better to know that he was not the only one in this stinking room who was afraid. Perhaps, he thought, they all are—afraid even in their sleep.

John, rushing with nausea, climbed down out of his bunk and ran along the dark corridor to the bathroom. In there it was brightly lighted and glaring white. He did not in his hurry see The Survivor.

When John was through he stood up and leaned weakly against the bulkhead, cold sweat running from his face. And he saw The Survivor, who was also being sick in one of the washbasins. The man could hardly stay on his feet and was clinging desperately to the shelf bracket above the basin. John went over to help him, and then he saw that the basin was running and stained with blood dripping out of The Survivor's mouth.

"I'll get the doctor," John said.

Finding strength somewhere, The Survivor swung around to face John, and the expression in his eyes was so wild and furious that John backed away.

The Survivor's voice was also furious and low. "Keep away," he said. "Don't get a doctor or anybody else. Just keep away. Leave me alone."

"I was scared, but you're sick," John told him.

The Survivor had to swing back to the basin. When he finished he turned again to John, and now his tone was different. He was almost pleading.

"Look," he said, "keep quiet about this, will you? If you tell the docs they'll ground me."

John was surprised. "You can't fly!"

There was again that sudden fury. "I can fly as well as you can, perhaps better."

"I didn't mean that. But you're sick. You're about to pass out right now."

"I'm all right," The Survivor said. "So just forget you saw anything."

John shrugged. "It's your funeral."

The Survivor looked at him with a curious, somber expression. "It's already been my funeral," he said. "Only I want a little more time to get there." He turned and washed his face and rinsed his mouth and turned back to John. "Just a little more time."

As they started back to the cabin together, John asked, "What's it like? In combat, I mean?"

"Just fly it and aim it the best you can," The Survivor said.

"Suppose you get scared?"

"It goes away when things really start. Just goes away. Then after it's all over, watch out. It comes back and you can goof."

"I hope I make it."

"You'll make it. You made it with the plane this afternoon so you'll make it."

"Are you really going up if there's a fight?"

"I'm going to try," The Survivor said.

John and The Survivor had just reached the cabin when reveille sounded. Over the speaker system, a raucous voice cried, "Chow down. Breakfast for all pilots."

John snapped on the overhead lights as the other two men in the cabin woke up. Strickland, the hairy one, looked at his watch and screamed. "What do they mean! It's one-thirty in the morning!"

"Oh, for the life of an aviator," Hendricks said.

"I can't eat breakfast at one-thirty in the morning," Strickland said.

"I can't either but I'm going to," Hendricks said. "I don't want to be up there with my guts growling so loud the Japs can hear 'em fifty miles away."

"Are we taking off in the dark?"

"Best time," John said, pulling on his trousers. "They can't see you."

"I can't seem them either," Strickland said. "How I get a medal and go home that way?"

"You don't," John said. "They send the medal home."
Strickland stood scratching his chest and looking at John.

"You don't understand the principles of war, friend," John told him. "Aviators are not wanted aboard carriers so—to get rid of us—they won't let us sleep; they're trying to wear us out. Because if there weren't any aviators on this ship, there wouldn't be any reason for it to be way out here in Indian country. It could be back Stateside, and they could use the flight deck for a dance floor. See?"

"I'm turning in my wings," Strickland said, scratching the bushy hairs on his chest.

"That where you keep 'em?" John asked.

"In here somewhere," Strickland said.

Hendricks said, "My stomach won't function at this hour of the night. How'd we get into this thing anyway? I'm not mad at anybody."

For the first time The Survivor said something. As he did they all turned to look at him, sitting weakly on his bunk. He looked pale and dead except for his eyes. "You better start getting mad," he said in a low voice. "It's healthier."

14

It was a long, grinding time until dawn. Twice the voice from the loud-speakers in the ready room called, "Pilots, man your planes." Twice they ran from the ready room and up to the long, pitching deck. In the dark they found their planes and were helped aboard by the plane captains, who also helped to strap them in. And then they sat in the parked planes with the wind whistling around them and the sky dark above them and waited for the order: "Pilots, start engines." But it didn't come that night, so after awhile they got out and went back to the ready room—to wait some more.

At last, at three minutes to five in the morning, the sun came up out of the eastern Pacific, and thus began a beautiful day for a fight. A gentle trade wind blew from the southeast and it was pleasantly cool—sixty-eight to seventy degrees Fahrenheit—with good visibility. From a plane in the sky you could see for fifty miles in all directions.

And at dawn on this June 4, 1942, the enemy launched his attack on Midway. From his four huge carriers he sent a wave of 108 planes winging toward the little island now marked by the long shadows of the rising run.

Against this attack the Marines on Midway could only muster twenty ancient old Buffalo fighters and six just as old and slow and clumsy Wildcats. This group, hopelessly outnumbered by far superior planes, were doomed from the moment of take-off. Within half an hour, seventeen of the twenty-six had been shot down and seven more planes ruined beyond repair. Of them all, only two would ever fly again.

This attempt by the Marine land-based aircraft to stop the enemy's attack totally failed so that at six-thirty in the morning the bombs began to fall on Midway. The Marine command post and the mess hall were destroyed, the powerhouse was hit hard as were the oil tanks and the seaplane hangar. Fires set the hospital and storehouses ablaze. The bombs, however, missed the runways and killed only a few men.

Now the Marines on Midway launched an air attack against the enemy carriers themselves. The first flight of six TBF Avengers and four Army B-26 Marauders tried to avenge the damage to Midway by making a torpedo attack on the enemy carrier *Hiryu*, but they were overwhelmed by enemy fighters. Five of the six TBFs were shot down and three of the B-26s, and no hits were scored.

The next wave of Marine and Army planes was also

stopped cold. Of sixteen SBD dive bombers, eight were shot down and six more ruined, one of them being hit 259 times although the pilot was not killed. In addition to these Marines losing their lives in low-level attacks, fifteen Army Flying Fortresses, safe at 20,000 feet above the enemy, dropped their bombs uselessly into the sea.

By eight-thirty in the morning of this bright and pleasant day, practically all of Midway's planes had been destroyed and most of its pilots were dead. The enemy had won this first round of the long battle.

15

And now, hardly five hours after take-off, the enemy's planes were back aboard their ships being rearmed with more bombs and being refueled for the second attack on Midway.

And this condition—flight decks crowded with unarmed planes—was exactly what the men on the U. S. Navy's carriers wanted. For they were on their way now; so many of them making the last flight they would ever make.

16

The first wave of U.S. planes took off from the carrier *Hornet*. First to leave were the fifteen planes of Torpedo Squadron Eight, each one armed with one aerial torpedo. Next came the thirty-five SBD dive bombers and after them the fighters. For a few minutes they circled over the ocean, forming up in groups of Vs, the low flying torpedo planes down near the sea, the dive bombers at 13,000 feet, and the fighters hovering protectively above them all. And then, at last, they turned and headed toward the enemy.

From above, the little group of fifteen torpedo planes low over the sea were almost invisible, their dark-blue camouflage paint blending almost perfectly with the blue of the sea itself. And because of this a great tragedy began to take form, for mile by mile the fighters and bombers high above the ocean began to pull away from the torpedo planes until at last they were alone down there and unprotected.

The second part of the tragedy blossomed now as the fighters and bombers, on the wrong course, missed the enemy entirely and flew far past him, finally landing on Midway itself.

And so the little group of fifteen torpeckers droned on above the slow waves, their shining discs of whirling propellers pulling them quickly to their destruction.

To the men of Torpedo Eight, the sight of the enemy when at last they found him was appalling. There on the sea ahead of them were four huge carriers, flight decks crowded with planes. Around the carriers were rings of anti-aircraft guns on battleships, cruisers and destroyers. And above the carriers were literally swarms of fighter planes— hundreds of them up there waiting and droning and waiting for the men of Torpedo Eight.

These thirty men of VT-8 in fifteen planes could have turned away from such a formidable enemy, turned and waited for fighter cover or simply turned away. But they did not turn. They had come a long way to fight and they must fight now or not fight at all.

Just before these men left their ship, the commanding officer of Torpedo Eight had said, "If there is only one plane left to make a final run-in, I want that man to go in and get a hit." And then the commanding officer had said, "May God be with us all."

That was the last thing he ever said.

To launch a torpedo from a plane you must fly it low and straight toward your enemy, and you must get close to him and then you drop it. Low and straight and level and steady. You need fighter planes to protect you when you do this, because you're a perfect target for guns and a sitting duck for enemy fighters who can swoop down on you and kill you.

Torpedo Eight had nothing to divert the gunners, nothing to keep the fighters off its back as on a crisp, clear June morning it dove down to a few feet above the sea and started what was to be its final run-in.

The tragedy would have been somewhat less terrible if Torpedo Eight had scored any hits on the enemy—even one. But none of the torpedoes dropped got home.

And one by one, the planes of Torpedo Eight were struck down. The guns got some of them, the fighters got the rest.

Of the fifteen planes of Torpedo Eight none survived. Of the thirty men of Torpedo Eight, twenty-nine died that day. Only one lived, and in the sea he had to hide under a seat cushion from the strafing of enemy fighters who wished to kill him also.

The enemy had won the second round.

17

By nine-thirty in the morning of June 4, the enemy could afford to feel triumphant. His great plan of conquest was working beautifully. With practically all the planes based on Midway now destroyed and the little island in flames, it would be a simple task for the enemy to move in his bombardment group of battleships, cruisers and destroyers and lying off the island beyond the reach of the coast defense guns, destroy them one by one with point-blank fire from the ships' rifles. Then there would be only the little detachment of U. S. Marines on shore left to defend Midway with small arms. A detachment which would surely be overwhelmed by the hordes of the enemy now waiting in their troop transports.

At nine-thirty in the morning the fall of Midway seemed as inevitable as the fall of Wake and the Philippines and Java had been, and all the rest of the islands the enemy had attacked since he began this war with the treacherous assault on Pearl Harbor.

But the fall of Midway was not the real reason the enemy had come into these waters. He was here to find and destroy the last fighting units of the Navy in the Pacific. So far the enemy had beaten off every attack by Marine and Army land-based aircraft without suffering any damage. And now he had killed thirty-six of the forty-one Navy carrier-based torpedo planes without a single torpedo reaching his ships.

The rest, the enemy thought, will be easy.

Only two things worried him a little. The attacks of the Navy torpedo planes had delayed the refueling and rearming of his planes, which were still on the decks of his ships, and these same torpedo planes had drawn his fighter protection down from its high altitude almost to sea level.

And so, although many gallant men died in those torpedo planes that morning, they did not die uselessly. Although they did not hit the enemy nor hurt him, they slowed his preparations to attack and they pulled the lethal Zeke-fighters down from the high sky, leaving it empty for what was coming.

18

"Pilots man your planes! Pilots man your planes!" the harsh and almost inhuman voice sounded from the loud-speakers.

A pilot sitting next to John in the ready room groaned, "Not again."

Another older pilot said, "I think this is for real."

And they all ran out of the ready room into the clear, bright, crisp air of the morning. In the flight suits with the navigation gear hanging around their necks, with Mae West life preservers on and heavy boots, with the big pockets stuffed with charts and pencils and a sandwich, with flight helmet straps flapping around their throat and mike cords streaming, they were an ungainly bunch of people, who at this time and place did not look dangerous. They looked in fact awkward and helpless and no more to be feared than a litter of puppies in a basket.

As John started up the ladder to the flight deck the pilot in front of him stumbled and fell. And couldn't get up.

"Help me," the pilot said to John.

It was The Survivor. His face was a dead gray in the early morning sunlight; he was sweating and pain was pulling the muscles of his neck into cords. His eyes were hot and wild.

"You're not supposed to go," John told him.

"Help me!" The Survivor said. He was not asking; it was a command.

John helped him get to his feet and on up to the flight deck. There The Survivor shook John's helping hands away and then pulled his helmet down close over his eyes. He staggered a little as he ran, his head down and his arm across his chest so that no one could read the faded gold letters of his name under the faded gold wings on his jacket.

John caught up with him and ran beside him to the waiting planes. "You'll be in trouble if they find out," John said.

The Survivor stopped at his plane and turned. "I don't want to die here," he said.

The Survivor's plane captain came up then and when he saw The Survivor he looked puzzled.

"He's sick, he's hurt," John told the plane captain. "He shouldn't go."

The plane captain looked hard at The Survivor. "Can you fly it, sir?" he asked.

The Survivor nodded.

"Good enough to get a hit, sir?"

The Survivor nodded again.

"Then let's go," the plane captain said, as he helped The Survivor get up on the wing and on into the cockpit.

But when The Survivor's gunner started to climb up on the plane, The Survivor ordered him down. "I won't need you," he told the gunner. "And you don't want to go where I'm going."

John ran on to his own plane where his gunner was also waiting.

"Good weather for squirrel shooting," the gunner said.

"The best."

"You okay, sir?"

"Nothing like a dunking to clear the head," John said climbing up on the wing.

He got down into the cockpit while his gunner climbed into the cockpit behind. The plane captain checked belts and harness and then climbed down off the wing.

John twisted around so that he could see his gunner. "They tell me it's going to be rough."

"I'm just going along for the ride."

John laughed—a little.

When he had finished his check-off he had time to look around. In the next plane on his right his brother Jeff was sitting, talking to his gunner. To his left The Survivor was slumped down in the cockpit so that the flight deck officer wouldn't recognize him. No gunner sat in the rear seat. And then plane by plane he looked at the faces of men he had known for a long time. Men who had been kids when they had first reported for flight training but although they still looked like kids, would become men on this morning— if they lived.

From the bullhorn the raucous voice cried, "Start engines."

One by one the engines coughed and sputtered and whined and started, the propellers beginning to turn, to jerk and stop and move again, and then turn and rev up and change from moving blades to motionless discs.

And then began the marvel of carrier take-off. The planes, wings folded upward, were parked as tightly as they could be parked on the after part of the flight deck. Engines were droning as the ship now ploughed into the wind, and the flight deck officer began the graceful routine of sending them off one by one, one after the other as fast as they could go. With his flag first waving ever faster around his head as a signal for the pilot to lower his wings and turn up the engine, he waited until in his judgment there was enough power now to roll the plane forward; power enough and lift to get it off the flight deck before it reached the end. When there was power enough he signaled with the flag to go, and the planes moved ahead one by one.

They moved so slowly and awkwardly at first, John thought, watching them going. Like big crippled birds, staggering, wings rocking, body swishing. But as they gathered speed, they lost the thing of the ground and became things of the air.

The prop blast of the planes taking off ahead of him rocked John's plane roughly and shook it like a dog with a bone. His own prop shone silver in front of him and also shook the plane as he held it there on the deck with his heels hard on the brakes.

He wasn't thinking about anything much now. Just the faintly sickening smell of the plane—the castor oil and hot engine and grease and paint. The 1000-pound bomb attached to the fuselage under him; that the paint was peeling on the wings and the white star; that the plane hadn't been swept out for a long time. John wondered about that. Where did all the dust and dirt come from? Out here at sea in the clean bright air? But there was always a layer of dust and dirt in the plane, and now it was quivering on the metal floor plates, tiny bits of dust dancing away down there between his feet.

And it was now his turn to go. He looked back once more to his gunner. "Shoot straight, Guns," he said.

"Fly good, sir. Don't worry about anything jumping you." The gunner patted the machine guns affectionately.

The flag signaled for him to go. John took his feet off the brakes and the plane lumbered forward. With the throttle jammed all the way forward and his gloved hand holding it there, he tried to keep the plane going straight down the deck toward the blue sea rising and falling at the end. For the first few seconds he felt almost helpless and as awkward as the plane, but as the speed increased and the wings began to lift a little, he felt his control of the plane come back.

When he reached the island of the ship John started easing back on the stick. The plane stayed ground-borne for a few more yards and then, with more back stick, she lifted her wheels from the wood and steel of the ship and was in the air and clear and going before the end of the flight deck flashed under her.

John was flying an SBD dive bomber, the old Douglas Dauntless—and dauntless they were. They were slow and, for airplanes, ugly—rough and awkward. They had none of the comforts of home or any place else; they were designed and put together to do one thing—dive bomb. They had no speed and could not go very high and were sitting ducks for fast fighters. But they could go straight down and they could go so far down—so close to a target—and still pull out without going into the sea that they were dangerous aircraft.

No one cared what they looked like because they were superb aircraft to handle. There was no treachery in the Dauntless, and you could call on it to do almost impossible things, and it would do them for you in an honest and straightforward fashion. You could punish them, and they would not turn on you and revenge themselves. You could have great chunks of your Dauntless shot away and still fly it home; the enemy could riddle it with bullets and somehow it would still fly.

It was now almost eight o'clock in the morning. John, flying at 19,000 feet, had formed up with his squadron and the other dive bombers. Far below him, and almost invisible against the blue sea, were fourteen of Torpedo Squadron Six's Devastators looking as though they were motionless, hung by invisible strings from the sky. John did not know it, nor did the men flying the Devastators then know it, but of the fourteen planes down here only four were going to live through this.

Above him, and clearly seen against the sky, were the fighters, the stubby little F4F Wildcats.

Behind him the flight deck of the *Enterprise* was fading away.

Ahead of him lay the enemy, waiting for him and ready and confident that John could not hurt him.

The Dauntless droned on and on. In the rear cockpit the gunner sat, his twin-mount 50-caliber machine guns unlimbered and ready, his eyes searching the sky for enemy fighters to fly down on him from out of the glare of the sun. The gunner was thinking about little things. The one tooth his son had had when he had last seen the boy—two years ago. He hoped the motionless man sitting only a few feet in front of him would consider his son when the time came. For the gunner wanted very much to see his son again and count the new teeth that had come since he had seen him last.

The gunner took his eyes off the sky for a moment to look at the hooded head of the man in front of him. He wondered a little about John. The lieutenant seemed to run out of luck more than anybody he knew. The gunner didn't think that the lieutenant chickened out and he knew that when things were right the lieutenant was as good a pilot as anybody in the squadron, even the skipper. He just ran out of luck too soon, too often.

Maybe this time, the gunner thought, his luck will hold. Because, man, if you ever needed your luck to hold this was the day.

John was thinking that if the enemy was where they thought he was, a lot of the planes around him were going to run out of gas before they could get back to the carrier. He kept leaning it out drop by drop, while at the same time he had to keep it flying in the formation of tight Vs.

John was flying right wing on his brother's plane, holding it in close, the wing tip of Jeff's plane only a few inches away from him. Flying left wingman was The Survivor. John looked over at him to see how he was doing and found him in that accustomed attitude of a pilot flying in formation. Motionless, head turned toward the lead plane, eyes fixed on it.

It was odd, John thought, that he didn't now feel afraid or even tense, although in an hour he would be in the first real combat he had ever seen. He wondered what it was going to be like to drop a bomb on an enemy ship with the purpose and intent of sinking it and the men who lived in it. But oddly, he thought about the enemy as a man not at all. Just a ship which soon he would see and attack. He would either hit it or miss it; and it would either hit him or miss him. But he wasn't as afraid now as he had been the night before throwing up in the toilet bowl.

He hoped the gunner was all right. He was a good gunner and a good man and he could shoot straight.

John wanted very much to bring that gunner back alive and unhurt when all this was over.

And so the twenty fighters and thirty-eight dive bombers and fourteen doomed torpedo planes moved toward the enemy ships. The sky was almost clear, only a few fluffy cumulus clouds hanging up there with the planes. From 19,000 feet John could see for fifty miles all the way around. Below him, the torpedo planes winging over it, the sea was calm with no visible whitecaps—just an enormous expanse of blueness. A beautiful day. If you had to die it was a nice day for it.

The gunner in the seat behind John kept swinging the machine guns around on the oiled steel track, checking to see that they moved easily, even against the blast from the propeller. They were good guns, and he had certainly babied them. So they swung and moved and aimed easily, and he went on to check the ammo. He didn't want anything to jam up on him this morning. He wanted those bright copper cases with their smooth bullets to go into the guns fast and in order and to come out empty, the bullets going where they were supposed to go and the empty cases flipping away into the sky and the sea. He hoped he wouldn't be as scared as he was now when he finally put his face down on these guns and pulled the triggers, and felt that old familiar pounding against his body and heard the oddly faint sound of it against the roar of the engine. He sure hoped he wouldn't get too scared or he'd miss.

Thus an hour passed with the pilots and the gunners and torpedo men sitting almost motionless in the planes, each thinking his own and private thoughts.

And another half an hour passed. John checked his chart. According to the chart the enemy was supposed to be below him right now, but the sea was blue and empty.

Ahead of him the group commander was also aware that the enemy was supposed to be here but wasn't. At this point in that flight on that morning, the planes had reached the limit of their fuel endurance. There was now exactly enough gas to get them safely back to their carrier.

The group commander recognized this problem and knew that he had a choice of two things: he could turn the squadrons back now, away from the enemy, and go home. Or he could fly on, hoping to find the enemy, and take the chance that some or all of them would not have gas enough left to reach the carrier.

The group commander decided to go on searching. For thirty-five more miles, gas in the tanks lowering with every one of them, he flew on, the squadrons in tight Vs following him.

And then down on the sea, they saw a single, white, straight, long trail—like a white pencil had been run across the blue water. At the head of this trail a ship as tiny as a pinhead was moving.

The group commander decided that this must be one of the enemy ships, and that it was going toward the rest of them, so he turned the air group and flew up the white trail and flew on into his destiny, leading the other pilots to theirs.

The enemy had won the first two rounds of the fight, and won them brutally. This was round three.

19

The dead pilots and crew men floating in that blue sea could never know what their utterly brave attacks on the enemy carriers had accomplished, nor how many lives they would save by giving their own.

But as John looked down at the enemy almost four miles below him, he saw three enemy aircraft carriers milling around, all of them out of formation so that each became a separate target, and all of them with their flight decks crowded with planes.

Down there, too, fighting now to climb up to and beyond the dive bombers were the fast enemy fighters—sleek little planes and deadly. Very fast and maneuverable with heavy firepower from both 20 mm. cannon and 7.7 mm. machine guns. Their only fault was their fragility—a good burst from a 50-caliber gun could ruin them.

These enemy fighters—Zekes they were called—had been

pulled down to sea level by the torpedo plane attacks so that John, and his brother, and The Survivor and the rest of the dive bomber pilots were able to approach the enemy without being molested and still under the cover of their own fighter protection, the stubby and tough little Wildcats now flying high above them and waiting for the Zekes to get up there.

The Zekes never got there. Picking out two of the enemy carriers, the thirty-seven dive bombers split into two groups and began the long, screaming dive.

For John now in these last seconds of straight and level flight, there was much to do—and no time left to think about anything else than his gunner, his plane, the bomb hanging below him and, far, far below, the enemy.

John turned on the mechanism for stick-firing of the fixed machine guns in the wings of the Dauntless. He pulled the bomb release so that when the time came the bomb would drop and, he hoped, hit. Then as he approached the turn-over point, he began opening the Dauntless' big flaps with the holes in them the size of basketballs. As he opened them, he anticipated the lift they would give him and held the plane level against it.

"You all set?" he asked the gunner.

"Set and ready, sir."

"If anything jumps us on the way down let me know, but there won't be much I can do about it," John told him.

"I'll take care of it, sir," the gunner said.

Ahead of him his brother's plane reached the range and vanished. Next The Survivor went down.

And now it was his turn.

John nosed the plane down sharply—ten, twenty, thirty degrees. The sea swung in front of him, vast and blue and empty. He pushed the plane down—forty, fifty, sixty degrees now. Still an empty sea.

At 280 knots he pushed it the rest of the way, and the Dauntless entered the last long phase of the attack heading down at a steep seventy degrees.

John and the gunner were hanging from the belts now as the plane went almost straight down. John braced his body with his elbows and knees and held her straight as the enemy carrier swung into the round ring of the bomb-sight. It swung out again. John corrected for this and watched the long thin deck of the carrier swing back into the ring. He held it there and watched it coming up toward him.

The dust which had danced on the metal floor of the plane now hung, oddly motionless, in the air around him. His flight suit floated out in front of him and something, he never found out what, fell out of one of his pockets and rattled down somewhere into the plane.

In the rear cockpit the gunner, swung around so that he was riding backward, was now jammed into his seat. His face was almost down on the guns as he swung them rest-lessly back and forth, searching the sky for enemy fighters but seeing only his own. They seemed to the gunner to be rising straight up as though on an invisible elevator.

It was a lonely way to do things, the gunner thought. Sitting here looking up at an empty sky while some guy you hardly knew was taking you right down the barrel of every gun on the ships below. Well, he thought, that's the way it goes.

Ahead of John his brother's plane and The Survivor's plane seemed not to be moving at all. The only thing that moved was the enemy carrier and the ocean—both of them rushing up toward him.

And then his brother's plane pulled out of it and John could see the bomb—a little black, fat cigar—falling straight on down. Around Jeff's plane the antiaircraft shells were bursting in strange slow-growing puffs of black smoke but Jeff's plane seemed unhurt.

But John could not watch it long—he must watch now only the ship below him.

The ship was the enemy aircraft carrier *Kaga*, which in the enemy's language means "Increased Joy." To John, as it rushed up toward him, it looked immensely dangerous. The antiaircraft guns were firing up at him with a deadly purpose, the flashes at the gun muzzles looking pale but mean in the bright sunlight. The flight deck looked very clean and the planes parked on the after end of it were in orderly rows almost like the toy soldiers he used to play with. As he came closer, he could make out men working around the planes and more men standing on the bridge of the island.

In the bow of the ship, painted on the deck, was the insignia of the enemy—the red ball of the rising sun which John and the rest called the meat ball. It made a good target and he held it in the bombsight as the ship began to turn, the white wake streaming away from it curving sharply and beautifully in the blue water.

The little black, fat cigar entered the ship with to John no sound at all. He thought, that's a direct hit. About as direct as you can make it, and he was glad that it was Jeff's bomb which had gone into the ship and disappeared somewhere inside it.

And then the explosion came. It was so huge and instant and violent that it startled John and in a moment violently buffeted his plane so that he had to fight to get the meat ball back in the bomb sight. There was a sudden spouting of black smoke and then flame and then white smoke streaked with dirty yellow.

"Jeff got a hit," John said to the gunner. "My brother got a hit!"

"You get one, too, sir," the gunner said, still sitting backwards and looking at the sky.

"In a minute," John said.

The gunner took a chance then and looked around and down. To him, who had not seen the ship rushing upward, the carrier looked as though it were only a few feet away. It froze him in his seat for a second and then he went back to his work. He thought: you know, it takes a few guts to dive on a ship the way the lieutenant is doing. Yes, it took a few.

Now John could see The Survivor's plane.

He watched it all the way down. The Survivor never swerved all the way. He made no attempt to pull out—just went all the way.

Antiaircraft hit him, tearing a wing off the Dauntless and spinning it almost all the way around, but The Survivor went on down, straight toward the carrier.

Guns hit him again and John wondered, watching him, if The Survivor was still alive. The ruined plane was no longer diving now, only falling, broken and awkward.

They hit him again and this time their gunfire blew the bomb loose from the plane, and it fell free and struck the carrier as The Survivor, still in his plane, struck the sea beside it with a white, clean splash of the blue water. It was like the headstone of a grave, John thought. Who could want anything better than that clean-rising white splash of water against the blue sea? It was a deep grave, John thought, 12,000 feet deep.

And now it was his turn. The altimeter needle was rolling

backward fast—8500 feet, 8300 feet, 8000 feet. He had now only a moment to give to himself and all he could think was: don't goof this.

But he *was* goofing it. The carrier below him was sliding away out of the bombsight. It felt to John as though he and his plane and his bomb had been frozen into some sort of invisible mass so that he could not move it, while the carrier, free on the sea, was escaping from the little circle of the bombsight.

He tried to twist the plane to catch the ship again—it slid fast through the sight and out the other side. John could feel sweat breaking on him now—the sweat of utter embarrassment. He was here to drop a bomb on a ship and he *could not do it*. He was caught in something; the ship was not. No matter how he moved the plane, the ship below him slid away as though it was moving and he was staying motionless.

The gunner felt the swaying of the plane and thought: the lieutenant is having trouble staying on target. But the gunner was sitting facing the sky and could not look forward and down to see what was the trouble.

The altimeter needle was spinning off the feet—it slid past 5000—and John knew that he had only seconds left now and 2300 feet to go before he would have to drop the bomb whether he was on target or not. At this speed he could not live if he let the plane go below 2700 feet—there simply would not be enough altitude left to pull it out before it struck the sea.

He could see the carrier outside the bombsight. It looked huge, the pall of smoke pouring out of it making it even larger, but it was still moving fast through the water, twisting and turning so that the white wake looped and curled. He could see the little figures of men standing on the bridge, their faces turned upward toward him. Other men, scurrying like little rats, were dragging long lines of fire hoses out across the flight deck, out of which smoke was pouring from the two great holes Jeff and The Survivor's bombs had torn into it.

Four thousand feet—1300 feet left, barely seconds of time—and the target had slithered out of the bombsight again and lay far to the right of it.

John wondered in his agony why he couldn't get on target and stay on? What force was holding the plane off of it? What was *against* him?

But he was not on, and the altimeter needle had dropped below 3500 feet and was spinning down to 3000.

He was trying hard when it happened. With the rudder and stick he was trying to swing the plane over to the carrier, to get it in the bombsight and hold it there long enough to give the bomb a steady and straight trajectory down to the target, when something hit the plane. It was as though it had been struck by an enormous hammer swung from the very top of the sky. It slammed John and the gunner hard against the cockpit wall and actually moved the plane sideways through the air. Instantly following the hammer blow the sky went black—as black as the darkest night; blacker. In this total darkness there was now a hard, acrid odor.

John heard the gunner's surprised voice say, "Wow!"

And then the plane crashed out of the blackness into the brilliant sunlight. John, pulling himself back into the center of the cockpit, looked through the bombsight.

The flight deck of the carrier below him was nailed in the sight, the cross hairs exactly and steadily in the center of it. The explosion of the antiaircraft shell so close beside his plane had physically shoved it over and lined it up with the target.

As the altimeter needle came to the 27 on the dial, John released the bomb. As soon as he felt it fall away he started the heavy, steady, slow backward movement of the stick and prepared himself for the slamming down into the seat the pull-out would cause. He prepared, too, for the draining of blood out of his brain so that for seconds he would be almost unconscious.

He would never see where the bomb went. Gravity was now collapsing his body; he could feel his blood and muscles and bones being forced downward. Ahead of him the bright sky was graying, the smoothly swinging blue sea was turning black. His legs and feet felt as though the surge of blood into them would break the skin and flow out of him.

The plane was thrown violently around by the bursting antiaircraft shells, and fragments of them were striking it, but John could do nothing against the force of gravity which held him motionless and almost blind in the seat.

And then he was in straight and level flight and the sky turned bright and blue again. Control of the airplane came back to him, and he began to swing it hard from side to side and at the same time to force it upward as fast as it would go.

The sound of the gunner's voice surprised him—like a voice from the sky—faint and far away.

"Oh, my God!" the gunner said.

"What's the trouble. You hurt?"

"You hit her," the gunner said. "Right through the flight deck. It . . . *there it goes.* A *beautiful* drop, Lieutenant."

John did not answer as he felt the wet hotness of his embarrassment flooding over his skin.

John did not want to look back to see what the bomb

had done. He felt completely detached from it now—as though he had not even brought it to that point and let it go. He thought: Let the bomb do what it is going to do.

He pushed the throttle all the way forward and fought his way upward through the gouts of antiaircraft fire, upward to the protection of the fighters hovering in the sky far above him.

"It's terrible," the gunner said. "I can't see for the smoke, but it's doing a lot of damage."

It did indeed do a lot of damage. John's bomb hit just forward of the *Kaga's* island, exploding as it tore through the flight deck. The blast destroyed the island from which the ship was controlled. It killed everyone on the bridge, including the captain, and below decks killed many more. It set the ship's fuel and the aviation gasoline afire so that in seconds the *Kaga* was a burning wreck.

"Let's get this crate home," John said, looking at the gas gauges. "If we can."

He looked up and was insulted by what he saw. The clean blue sky with the clean, white and drifting clouds was pocked and littered with dirty splotches of brownish smoke. And as he looked more of the splotches appeared bursting in salvos. Planes flew among these things, reeling and swirling.

The gunner sat facing aft, the machine guns ready. The smoking, flaming carrier was dropping away fast now, the plane again in clean flight as it fought its way upward toward safety. If only nothing jumps us now, the gunner thought, we've got it made in the shade. The lieutenant had flown it well, he thought, and had gotten a big hit. Now, please, let the lieutenant go on flying well and they would get home again. Fly it well. Fly it well.

But it was all too easy, the gunner thought, just to fly

out here and dive, and let go a bomb and hit a ship, and fly back and land and go below for chow and a little sack time before you had to get up and fly again. Too easy.

And he was right.

Swirling down, like symbols of fury, four of the enemy Zekes came at them. At first they looked to the gunner like black, short pencil lines with a black period in the center, but as they bored in they grew into planes—four of them.

The gunner put his face down on the guns and swung them toward the planes so that the round ringsight held on them.

"Four Zekes coming in," he said to John.

"After us?"

"Nobody else," the gunner said.

The four planes tilted in the sky so that the sun shone on the red meat balls and then swung back, almost like the pendulum of a clock. Now they were directly behind the SBD and overtaking fast.

The gunner flipped the safety off and fingered the ammo and held tightly to the guns.

And then to his left, two more Zekes appeared, joining up with the others.

"Two more," he said to John.

"Now it's your turn," John told him.

Yeah, the gunner thought, my turn. What could he do against six of them? He'd heard a lot about these enemy fighters with not only 7.7 mm. machine guns in the wings but the big 20 mm. cannon. What could he do with 50-calibers against all that?

"Are we going to get any help?" John asked him.

"Don't see any," the gunner said, searching the sky for the blue-gray fighters and not finding any.

John strained against the harness holding him in the seat and looked back.

It was appalling. The six planes swirling toward him looked so vicious, so deadly—and so impersonal. Just guns flying toward him and overtaking him. In a moment, he knew, the straight edges of the twelve wings would begin to blink. Bright little flashes shimmering along all those wings. Then the shells would come into his plane, ripping up it.

John looked upward and found nothing. None of his friends in the stubby Wildcats were swooping down to help him. They couldn't—they were busy helping someone else.

John looked forward again just in time to see a plane reeling downward toward him. Flame and smoke streamed from it and pieces of it came away and floated down, slipping and sliding like falling leaves.

As it flashed past, John looked over and saw Strickland still in the cockpit, his gunner dead behind him. Strickland looked exactly as he did asleep with the fan stirring the hairs on his chest. He was lying over in the side of the cockpit, his head resting against the cowling, his eyes closed.

First, The Survivor, John thought, and then Strickland and then—him? And then how many others? Jeff?

"They've opened up," the gunner said.

John knew his only chance was to get down on the deck. With the enemy's guns fixed in the wings they would have to get down there with him to hit him, and maybe he could get down closer than they could. One thing about the old SBD, at least you knew where it was when you flew it, and it was always honest.

Little streams of light were going past him and once past seemed to slow down and grow tired and curve and fall.

John pushed the Dauntless over and down. It caught the

gunner by surprise and jammed him back into his seat, almost pulling his hands away from the gun. As the plane went almost straight down, the gunner looked up and saw the six Zekes flash by. It was too late, he knew, to fire but he fired anyway, to feel that good, solid pounding of the gun.

"Hit anything?" John asked him.

"Just warming her up," the gunner said.

The blue sea was rushing toward him while above, the Zekes swirled around and down and took up the chase.

John leveled off just above the waves and looked back.

The Zekes were coming in again, the wings winking their little lights.

At first he didn't know what had happened. The plane lurched, and then he felt a hard thud against his shoulder—like a blow with a boxing glove; not, as he had imagined, the penetration of a piece of metal through his flesh and bone. Just a thud.

They hit the gunner, too.

A 7.7 mm. bullet ripped up his right arm from wrist to elbow but the guns saved his life. The 20 mm. slug hit the gun mount, the explosion ripping the guns loose.

Ordinarily it took two men to lift and carry these heavy twin-mount 50-caliber machine guns, but now as they were blown free of the ring mount, the gunner, with one arm shattered by the 7.7 mm., held them as a man would hold a light rifle. He laid them down on the rim of the cockpit and sighted along them and fired at the Zeke coming straight up behind him. He just held the trigger down and clung to the guns and blew the Zeke out of the sky.

That was all he could do. With a sort of gentle clumsiness and a good-by, he let the guns go and watched the white splash they made vanishing behind him.

John now found that his left arm wouldn't move. It didn't

hurt, but it wouldn't move. He glanced at his shoulder and was surprised to see all the blood and the torn cloth and the shreds of <u>meat</u>. He was more surprised at the absolute whiteness of the broken bones sticking out of his flight suit. They didn't even seem to be his bones.

"You okay?" he asked the gunner.

"No," said the gunner, "the gun's gone."

This was bad. It made John feel somehow naked and helpless.

"I'm hit," he said.

"I know," the gunner said. "Your blood is all over the place. How bad is it, Lieutenant?"

"I don't know. I don't feel anything."

"Neither do I. . . . Here they come again."

"Our only chance is to get right on the deck and slow her down. If I lose her. . . ."

"The taxpayers can buy us a new one."

John nosed the SBD closer to the water and then, holding the stick between his knees, reached the throttle with his right hand and slowly, slowly eased it back. As the plane slowed down it grew heavy in his hands and resentful. It was not made to fly this way with barely enough lift in the wings, barely enough air stream for control. It sank, tail first, toward the sea but John eased the throttle forward enough to hold her there, dragging along inches above the waves.

The Zekes came in again, low and fast behind him.

"I dropped the gun," the gunner said. "They knocked it loose and I couldn't hold it."

With his left hand the gunner reached around and got the 38-caliber Smith & Wesson revolver out of a shoulder holster. As the Zekes poured in toward them, he aimed and fired at the closest one, the little pistol popping sharply with little puffs of smoke which instantly vanished. He fired six times and then threw the empty pistol up at a Zeke as it roared over him, the spinning propeller forcing him to duck his head. The pistol hit the bottom of the fuselage, skinning off an inch of paint, and then fell down into the sea.

The Dauntless seemed to be hanging by invisible wires just above the water and to be dragged along by these wires.

John watched his gauges steadily, watching the laboring engine beginning to heat up—the oil temperature needle sliding across the dial. He cranked hard on the cowl flap handle but they would open no wider. Nor would the wing flaps with their Swiss cheese holes. The trim tabs could do nothing more for him.

The oil temperature needle slid slowly into the red danger band as the Zekes turned and swooped down once again.

The gunner looked over the side and was amazed. The plane wasn't two feet above the waves, and once he felt a wave top slap against the after section. It was, he thought, as good as the lieutenant, or anybody else, could do—but it couldn't go on much longer. Already he could smell the engine heating up.

John could smell it too, and hear it beginning to labor and feel it beginning to lose power.

But the Zekes couldn't get down low enough to hit him. First the streams of tracers went over his head—bright little flames and then flying balls of bright dimming flame. Then the planes roared over him, their wheels neatly tucked up under them like gulls flying.

When they were gone, wheeling up to try again, John gunned the engine hard, the lift of the flaps zooming him upward.

"Here they come again," the gunner said.

John slowed it and dove for the water.

"They're going to try diving on us," the gunner said.

That way, John thought, they can hit us. If he held down too close to the water he would be trapped, unable to twist and turn away from them, for any turn where he was now would put a wing tip into the waves and dump the plane. But if he climbed for turning room and one of the Zekes came up his tail, it would be just as bad.

He looked up at the Zekes wheeling like incredibly swift buzzards above him. They were peeling off now, one after the other, swooping down toward him like death itself.

The gunner was watching them too. Now he didn't even have the pistol. He thought for a moment of throwing the 50-caliber machine gun shells at them and then slumped down in the cockpit.

He ought, the gunner thought, to be thinking Big Thoughts now. But he wasn't. He was just sitting there looking up at death and destruction swarming down on him and thinking: well, in a little while I'll be dead. No more. Just that.

They came down, the six of them, and the gunner was so absorbed by them that John's voice in his earphones surprised him.

"Let me know the second they open up."

"Aye, aye, sir," the gunner said, surprised at his own formality. What a way, he thought, to say "okay."

Then the enemy's wings began to flicker. The gunner said, "They're shooting."

John flung the old SBD forward with a shove on the throttle which almost bent the arm. At the same time he put it into as steep a turn as he dared, feeling the plane sinking out from under him and falling toward the sea.

He caught it at wave top level, rammed it upward a little way and flung it into another hard turn to the right.

The gunner was being slung this way and that against his harness, saying to himself, "Fly her, Johnny. Fly her. Fly the wings off her, Johnny."

And then, as the plane slammed over into another hard turn and the wing tip grazed the seeking waves, the gunner suddenly wondered if he had said all that out loud. Calling a lieutenant Johnny. Man, they could take you to the mast for that.

The gunner looked down at his microphone and said out loud and slow, "Fly her, Johnny!"

"Okay, Guns," John said. It was a good feeling to know that the gunner was back there. And it made him feel good to have the gunner call him Johnny, instead of Lieutenant this and Lieutenant that.

They couldn't hit him. And as the six Zekes, pulling out of their steep dive upon him, struggled upward again, the Wildcats came down and caught them and slaughtered them.

For a few minutes it was almost worse, John thought, than being shot at. Zekes and parts of Zekes and pilots in parachutes were falling all around him so that he had to twist and wrench the SBD through the air to avoid them.

And then suddenly he was alone.

"Guess it's over," the gunner said. "Don't see a thing."

"You complaining?" John asked.

"That's why I joined the Navy," the gunner said. "So I could complain on Government time."

John had heard that one a hundred times but now it seemed funnier than anything he had ever heard. He began to laugh and he could hear the gunner laughing, too.

"How bad are you hit?" John asked him when he could stop laughing.

"It won't get me Stateside."

"Mine either." John looked again at the shattered bones sticking out of his flight suit. "Bones sure are white, aren't they?"

"Yeah, and clean," the gunner said. "Are we going to make it back to the ship, sir?"

John looked at the gas gauges and felt as though icicles had been driven suddenly into his stomach. "Gas is pretty low," he told the gunner. "And we've been gone a long time."

John flipped on the automatic homing device which would lead him directly back to the *Enterprise*, and nothing happened. Examining the radio controlled device he found a neat round bullet hole squarely through the heart of it.

He was now faced with the grave problem of finding his way to safety by arithmetic. If in all the limitless miles of that ocean he could not find his ship, or any ship, he and his gunner were as surely doomed as if they had been destroyed by enemy antiaircraft shells or shot down by enemy fighters.

And the sea below could be so *empty* when your gas gauge needles were falling back toward zero and you had reluctantly switched over to the last tank in the plane.

Now he was beginning to hurt as he held the stick with his knees while he reached for the chart board with his right hand. A terrible, erratic throbbing had begun in his left shoulder, sending waves of pain so great through him that he felt as though one of them might drown him entirely.

"I got to do it by the numbers," he said to the gunner.

"Point Option." He didn't know why they called it that.

Before take-off John and the rest of the pilots had been given Point Option in the ready room. On paper it was simple. You took off and flew so many miles on such and such a course and then turned around and flew back. In the meantime your carrier had been steaming on a set course at a certain speed. On paper, all you had to do, was to draw a line along the carrier's course and pick off the speed at thirty-minute intervals. Then you could set your own course and fly back, and when you got to Point Option there she was, a matchstick down there on the water, with a long, thin white tail streaming out behind her.

On paper.

Point Option had been given to him as course 240, speed twenty-four knots.

John looked at his chart. Suppose the ship had not made good that fast twenty-four knots. If he flew for that course and speed and nothing was there, he and the gunner would never find the Big E. And how could the Big E make good twenty-four knots heading almost due west when the wind was from the east and very light at that. At each take-off and landing—for the combat air patrol groups and the anti-submarine groups—the ship would have to turn completely around and steam at maximum speed on a course of ninety degrees. How could she make up for all that lost time and distance?

John bet his life and the gunner's that she could not. He cut the carrier's speed in half and estimated a new Point Option along a line of 240 degrees, speed twelve. He set his course for this.

A lot of the other pilots, faced with the same problem, failed to solve it and were forever lost, their planes finally running out of gas and falling into the empty and implacable sea which took their lives—some immediately, some after days and nights of helpless floating.

John found his best altitude and then, like a surgeon working to save a dying patient, he went to work on the plane. He trimmed that plane until he eliminated every ounce of drag it was possible to lose. With his eyes fixed on the gauges, he leaned out the Pratt & Whitney engine like a miser giving away gold, feeding it just enough gas to keep him air-borne and the engine cool and not a drop more.

But the gas gauges kept steadily falling back toward the little "Empty" pins as he droned slowly across the sea toward an imaginary point on the ocean where he hoped his carrier would be.

20

On the aft end of the flight deck Lt. (j.g.) Conklin had been crying all day. Not tears. Just in his heart. He stood there with his little bright flags and looked out into the sky, the cruel sun flaying the flaming skin off him. His eyes were red and hurting from looking; he was sick from the beating of the sun, and he was crying for the friends of his who he knew would never come back to be waved aboard to safety by his little flags.

Fourteen of the dive bombers never came back to Conklin's flags. Ten of the big-bellied torpeckers never came back, and one of the little bumblebee Wildcats didn't make it.

Any man would cry in his heart.

On the carrier *Hornet* men waited, too, looking up into the sky and waiting for the far hammering of the planes as they came back. And as they waited all day for the planes of Torpedo Squadron Eight to appear in the sky, they, like Conklin, cried, for none of Torpedo Eight's planes were ever seen again. A dozen of Fighting Eight's planes with their pilots were lost.

And on *Yorktown*, doomed herself to die that day, all but one of her torpedo bombers died, and three fighters and two dive bombers.

On the bridge of the *Enterprise* the captain sat slumped in the high swivel chair and looked out through the tinted glass at the empty, empty sky. There were many other men and officers on the bridge with him, and yet the captain was all alone.

So far, the Battle of Midway was only a jumble of voices, flat and impersonal over the radio circuits. Bits and pieces of information had floated over the air to him and as he slumped in the chair, he tried to make a complete picture of them but he could not.

He sat trying to separate what he *knew* from what he guessed, from what he wished. There were, he *knew* now, at least four, perhaps five enemy carriers threatening him. They had been attacked by both Army and Marine land-based aircraft, but no damage had been reported so he must assume that they were all still afloat, undamaged, infinitely dangerous to his own ship.

Why, the captain wondered, hadn't some damage reports come in from the torpedo bomber strike launched so long ago? *Enterprise, Hornet* and *Yorktown* had sent forty-two torpedo planes against the enemy, piloted by the best naval aviators in the fleet. What had happened to them?

"Overdue and presumed lost." He hated the phrase but he could not avoid it. The torpedo bombers were long overdue; he *must* presume them lost.

And so there were still four—or five—large enemy carriers ranged against him now, and he had lost one of his most deadly weapons—the torpedo planes, which with one hit alone could sink any ship the enemy had.

The captain was afraid of another thing. Point Option had been set for the pilots that morning on a course of 240 and a speed of twenty-four knots. *Enterprise* had made good on the base course, but the light easterly airs had forced the Captain to turn his ship off the course too many times so that he had made good only twelve knots along the 240 degree line. Returning pilots using the original Point Option were, he knew, going to be trapped by two factors— time versus distance.

21

John Lawrence, in the crippled SBD, was now beginning to feel the jaws of this time-distance trap closing as he droned on and on above the sea. And a third jaw was closing too.

A little while ago he had been shocked and appalled when for some reason he had glanced down into the cockpit and seen the blood. It was everywhere. It bubbled up out of his flight boot; it streamed down his leg; it lay shimmering on the metal floor; his lap was soaked with it. How, he wondered, could a man have so much blood?

And more important right now, how could a man lose so much blood?

He was thinking about this as he flew the plane straight and level and slow, feeding it only enough gas to keep it flying on course and holding its altitude of 3000 feet.

In the back seat the gunner, facing forward now, was rigid against the waves of pain hammering inside his body and washing against his brain. He sat up as straight as he could, afraid that if he slumped in the seat as he wanted to do the waves would take him. So sit up straight and pay attention.

It was a pity, John thought, as he held the stick steady against the racking waves of pain, that after all he and the gunner had endured that morning they were going to be defeated by such ordinary things as time and distance.

He looked down at his shoulder and saw the blood streaming out the way muddy water used to finally stream out of holes in his little dams across the creek.

It was funny, John thought, how his life was running out through that hole.

He clamped the stick between his knees and pressed his gloved right hand against the hole. In a little while the blood began to ooze out between his fingers, and nothing he could do could stop it. He needed a stopper. If he could only reach the carrier, the medics could plug up this hole and the one in the gunner. The doctor, with the clean mask on him, would bark, "Stopper!" and a white-gowned medical corpsman would hand him a big stopper just the way they did it in the movies, slapping the big stopper with the long beaded chain on it right into the medic's hand so he would *know* he had a stopper in there.

A thin, tiny voice from far away said, "Hey, Lieutenant. Hey, Johnny!"

Where, John wondered, was that coming from? Or had he heard it at all?

The tiny voice said, "Hey, Lieutenant We're going straight down. You want to go straight down?"

"Say again," John said.

Then he looked up and was instantly terrified. The plane was going straight down toward the ocean. In sick dismay he realized that he had lost it. That he had been dreaming—no, he had been doping off again—and had lost it.

He didn't remember moving or thinking or doing anything but he knew later that he must have because the flaps went down, the throttle forward, the stick hard back, the pitch full.

It was so close the gunner couldn't bear to watch it and closed his eyes and prayed. When at last he opened them, the plane was climbing out of the reach of the sea, clawing back up into the air.

John almost cried in shame. Why, *why*? did he always goof things up? that little stunt had cost him gasoline that might cost him and the gunner their lives. WHY?

22

Conklin, his flags limp at his sides, looked always out into the sky, his bloodshot eyes hidden behind the enormous wrap-around dark glasses he had to wear to keep the sun from frying the eyes right out of their sockets. He looked and listened and heard at last the hard, dry, flat hammering of a plane. A different sound from that of the combat air patrol droning endlessly far above the ship. This was the sound of a plane at low altitude with its engine leaned out so thin he wondered how the pilot, whoever he was, could keep it in the air.

Then he saw it and his heart actually sank, his whole body feeling as though it would crumble down into a heap.

The plane—an SBD—was not flying at all; it was staggering along nose high, tail dragging, propeller flailing at the air. It was, Conklin knew, going to stall any second now. Stall and begin a slow short spin and go into the sea.

But the plane kept dragging itself toward the ship inch by inch. As it turned to get in line astern, Conklin held his breath for the turn was infinitely bad and infinitely dangerous. But somehow the SBD survived it and straightened up and began the last long staggering toward the flight deck.

"This is going to be tough," Conklin said into his mike. "Keep clear up there forward of the barrier. Fire fighters and medics better stand by."

Conklin now stepped out onto the flight deck, going so far out that he was beyond his shield. The thirty-five knot wind swept against him, but he braced his feet against it and stood there, wanting to be sure the pilot could see his flags.

Now he could see the number.

John Lawrence.

And no tail hook. Conklin could see it tucked up in its sheave.

And no wheels. They, too, were tucked up against the belly of the plane.

And the man at the radio who could so easily call out to John and tell him to get those wheels down and tail hook out just had to sit there, radio silence clamped on him so that the enemy could never hear his voice and take a bearing on him and so find his ship. Just sit there and watch this airplane coming in to sure destruction upon the flight deck.

But slowly the wheels came down, the hook appeared.

"Good boy!" Conklin said out loud, his cracked mouth smiling suddenly, the smile breaking the thin skin and letting tiny creases of blood appear.

It was the best landing John Lawrence ever made. His wheels touched and bounced a little; the tail hook caught the number two wire and brought the plane to a stop. He cut the ignition, and the propeller windmilled for a few

turns and stopped. Then it was quiet on the flight deck
and for a second, not a man moved.

Then, like a horde, they ran toward the plane—corpsmen
with stretchers, doctors, fire fighters in thick asbestos suits
galumphing along, dragging the hoses or carrying the foam
bottles, the plane captain (who carefully counted the fifty-
five bullet holes he found in the wings and body of his
SBD and who hours later called other men to see that Lt.
Lawrence had gotten his plane back with exactly two gallons of gas left in her) jumping up on the wing root.

Down in the wardroom the long dining tables were waiting
for the wounded, the doctors and corpsmen in their white
gowns waiting.

They laid John down on one table, the gunner on another
and clustered around them. The captain came down from
the bridge, hoping that John could tell him something of
the battle, but he was too late. John could only whisper
something about a stopper, a stopper with a long beaded
chain.

23

That was the end of the Battle of Midway for John
Lawrence, his SBD and his gunner.

But it was not the end of the battle. For three more
days the ships and planes of the enemy and the ships and
planes of the U. S. Navy slugged it out.

The enemy had come from his Empire just for this en-
counter. He had wanted to force us to fight and he had
done it. He had lured all the remaining strength of the
Navy in the Pacific, which he had so horribly crippled by
his sneak attack on Pearl Harbor, to come out to meet him

while he had overwhelming odds in ships and planes and brute force.

He was to regret it.

The pilots from *Enterprise* and *Hornet* and *Yorktown* mauled him. After the slaughter of our torpedo bombers, the enemy felt that he was invincible and found out that he was not.

His carriers went down one by one—*Soryu*, *Hiryu*, *Akagi*, and *Kaga*. The cruiser *Mikuma*, which had helped to sink the Navy's cruisers *Houston* and *Perth*, went down, and the cruiser *Mogami* was so crippled that she could not sail again for a year. Two hundred and seventy-two of the enemy's planes were destroyed with hundreds of pilots and thousands of the ships' company.

For the first time in a hundred years the enemy had been beaten. His bloody march across the Pacific toward the shores of the United States had been met and stopped and driven back.

This was the Battle of Midway.

PART TWO

THE SURVIVOR

1

As the hospital plane curved in low over Honolulu, John looked out the window at Pearl Harbor and the air station on Ford Island.

The last time he'd seen Pearl Harbor he had not thought that they could ever clean up the slaughter of the sneak attack. The whole harbor had been one great ruin, Ford Island a blasted and destroyed place. Now as he looked down at Ford Island, he saw a busy little Jeep with a big sign reading FOLLOW ME running around on the strip.

Below in the water, the battleships still lay, forever destroyed. The little waves of the harbor washed over the decks of the broken *California*. The round, helpless bottom of the battleship *Oklahoma* was a mound of red rust. The great, graceful bow of the *Nevada* still stuck skyward as though trying to pull the rest of the ship out of the deep mud of the harbor.

In the bucket seat next to him, the gunner said, "End of the line, Lieutenant. If we don't see each other again I'd just like to tell you I . . . well, I liked serving with you. And if I get into any more trouble I hope you'll be there."

"We'll see each other again, Guns," John told him.

"They'll patch us up and maybe we'll even get one of the new dive bombers—real hot."

"Yeah," the gunner said, knowing that they would not, ever, fly together again. "But I'll miss that old SBD. Just like home and fireside, that airplane."

What was the use, the gunner thought, of telling him? Let somebody else do it. Somebody who had never flown with the lieutenant in combat, somebody who had never had to wipe the lieutenant's blood off his face so he could see, somebody who didn't know the lieutenant. Because when they told him it was going to take the lieutenant apart. I mean, *apart.*

The gunner would fly again. Back in the rear seat with the twin-mount fifties shiny and ready to go. He wondered who his next pilot would be and hoped that when everything was down on the green baize the way it had been at Midway, his next pilot would be a little like the lieutenant. Let him goof when it didn't count. But when it did count. . . .

2

Sweat poured off John Lawrence. Not the sweat of hard work but the sweat of agony. As his left hand gripped the handle and pulled and the rope slid around the sheave and the heavy weight rose up the tracks, it felt as though knives were being drawn along the muscles of his left arm and left shoulder.

The pretty nurse came across the grass toward him and said, "That's good, John."

"Yeah," he said, discouraged by the never-ending pain.

"There's somebody to see you," the nurse said.

John turned loose the grip, letting the weight fall, and turned around.

His brother looked as lean and gray and taut as a fiddle string. His eyes were way back in his head, his skin stretched so tight that it looked as though the sharp bones would cut through it.

The pretty nurse stood for a moment looking at John. In a way she loved him, even though she knew that to him she didn't really exist. Nothing existed for John but to get back into an airplane. For weeks as his wound had slowly healed, she had patiently listened to him talk about getting back into an airplane.

Then the pretty nurse felt the warmth of tears coming suddenly and without warning, and she turned away from John so he wouldn't see.

How was he going to take it? she wondered. And that made her wonder how any of them could stand the things this war was forcing on them. How could they *endure* it? How could John even *want* to get into another airplane—ever? And yet once he had cried. It had been in the middle of the night, and she had held his hands while he cried—because his wound was healing so slowly; because it was keeping him away from an airplane.

"Hello, Johnny," Jeff said.

John wiped the sweat off his face with his sleeve. "Hello, Jeff. What's the matter, don't they feed you on the Big E any more?"

"If I had a pretty nurse to feed me with a spoon. . . ."

They watched the pretty nurse walking away from them.

"I'm ashore for some replacement pilots," Jeff said. "I'm group commander."

John thought of that day now so long ago and then made

himself stop thinking about it. "El groupo. On the *Enter-prise?*"

"Where else? She's a good old boat."

"When?"

"Oh, we'll train here for a couple of weeks and then go aboard. Most of the guys're fresh from Stateside."

"I'll be well by then. The doc said so."

John looked at his brother, wondering why he didn't seem very happy to hear this. And then a thought hit him like a hammer. "You're going to have a place for me, aren't you, Jeff? I mean, after all, you're the group commander. You can have anybody you want to fly your planes for you, can't you?"

"Yeah," Jeff said. Maybe, Jeff thought, after all it could be better to let the doctor do it or even the pretty nurse. It was a terrible thing to have to do to your brother. But then. . . .

"Look," Jeff said. "I'm going to hit you right in the face with something you're not going to like."

John stood looking at him. And he knew. He hoped that he was wrong, but he knew that he was not. So why make it so hard on Jeff? "I'm grounded," he said. "For how long?"

He expected to see relief in Jeff's eyes but there was none. "How long?" Jeff asked, his voice a little vacant.

John could feel the anger getting hot in him and he tried to cool it off. "Maybe for a month or so? I'll just lie around Waikiki with the *wahines.*"

The look in his eyes hurt Jeff so that he didn't have the courage to come right out with it. "You want to know what the doctor said, John? He said that ordinarily you would have been retired with a wound like that but there's a war."

Under the tan John's face turned gray and his eyes grew wet. "I can't fly again—ever?"

All Jeff could do was nod.

The anger flamed up and shot all through him. And bitter resentment. Why should they do this to him? Hadn't he hit a carrier? Hadn't he brought his gunner and his plane back? Didn't he have a Navy Cross and a Purple Heart in a pretty little box? What more could they want?

"You got hit pretty hard, Johnny."

"I can do anything in a plane with this arm I could ever do. I can bend a throttle over the stop just as far as you can."

John jerked his left arm violently around and the sudden, jolting pain almost made him faint. Jeff wanted to catch him and hold him steady but he knew his brother too well for that. He just stood there and let John fight back the pain until he could talk again.

"I'm resigning," John said.

"You can't resign. They won't let you, Johnny."

"They! *They!*" John said bitterly.

"I've got a job for you," Jeff told him.

"A job? What can I do? I'm just a punk out of high school and all I know how to do is drive an airplane."

"Air Group Operations officer," Jeff said.

John said angrily and bitterly. "What do I know about paper-pushing?"

"It takes a hundred men to put one pilot in the air. You're going to be one of them."

John said mockingly, "They also serve who only stand and wait. If I'm not fit to fly I'm not fit for anything."

His gaunt brother looked at him with grave and sunken tired eyes. "Stop crying, Johnny. There's a lot of war out there."

"All right," John said quietly, "what do I do?"

3

This terrible and bloody war roared on. The enemy had been stopped in his advance across the Central Pacific, but he had not been stopped in the south. Like an enormous octopus creeping over the sea bottom he was moving eastward, island after island. He had lost a tentacle at Midway, but his other arms were moving on, destroying everything they touched.

John felt somehow that the war was swirling away without him. That he was not even a small part of it. That he was left out; unneeded, unwanted.

He and his brother returned to the carrier *Enterprise* late in July, flying aboard with the replacement pilots—young men, really almost boys, to take the place of the men, now legend, who had lost their lives stopping the enemy at Midway.

The old ship hadn't changed at all. The same terrible, thick air at night; the same sounds and smells and peeling paint. Only one thing seemed different to John—there was a feeling in the ship now of experience. She and her crew had fought, and fought well, and could fight again. Only the new pilots would now be beset by the double problem all men going into combat for the first time must face: what will the enemy do? and more important, what will I do in the face of the enemy? Will I be brave or will I turn and run and be a coward? New men don't know; the others did, so that on the *Enterprise* the combat veterans had only to find out what the enemy was going to do. They *knew* what they would do when the time came because they had done it before—stand and fight.

The first time John went up to the familiar ready room, his old shipmates had greeted him and taken him back into the unacknowledged and almost secret society of pilots; the men of the ship for whom the ship was built and is now where it is. John was wearing his wings (the gold tarnished and giving evidence of his time at sea) as he had a right to do, even though he would not be allowed to fly, and the other pilots took him back. But as they found out that he had been grounded and wasn't really one of them any more, things changed.

They didn't become his enemies nor even strangers; it was just that they moved and lived in a different world— the world of sky and altitude and castor oil smells—the world of the pilot sustained by a machine in the air against all the laws of gravity. John was no longer in this world, that's all. He was a member of the air group; he was the Operations officer and actually knew more about the war than the pilots did, but this didn't change the one big fact: he was now no longer a pilot, no longer one of them and so more than ever John felt left out, abandoned, unneeded. In time he did not go into the ready room unless his duties took him there. It was the club, the secret meeting place, the house in the tree, the hidden cave of the pilots. If you weren't a pilot you weren't really welcome there.

On his first day aboard John had automatically lugged his gear below to his old cabin, with the bunk under the catapult sheave. As he came in and dumped his gear on the deck, four strangers looked at him, surprised and puzzled, for there were only four bunks in there.

Somehow he had expected to find the men with whom he had shared this place so long before. He realized now he had forgotten that they were dead—killed at Midway. Hendricks and Strickland and The Survivor with whom he had lived in this little steel-walled room. Now he was "the survivor" and these four men were strangers.

"Guess I got the wrong deck," John said, picking up his gear.

Alone in the corridor outside he checked his assignment sheet, running his eyes down through his battle station and wardroom seat and section, abandon ship station to his bunk assignment.

It was down in the bowels of the ship. When at last he found it, he was sweating and tired, the weight of the gear pulling against the injured muscles of his shoulder and making them start that drawn-out and nagging pain.

Perhaps it would not have hurt him so much if he had not been physically hurting, or if he had been warned. But now it hurt and humiliated him and made him feel even more left out and abandoned.

The cabin to which he was assigned was so small that the jaygees in it had to play cards on a piece of plywood resting on their knees. As John came in they looked up at him affably enough and welcomed him, although it was evident to him that the welcome was a little forced, as the three knew that a fourth would only crowd the tiny space allotted them a great deal more.

As John introduced himself he noted the new, pressed uniforms which said so clearly that these three were fresh from Stateside and had never been in combat. He noted, too, that on the shiny shirts there were no wings and this hurt him. Why couldn't he have been assigned to a cabin with pilots, he wondered bitterly. Why with these men whose duties had nothing to do with the air group, for two of the jaygees were communicators who a great deal of the time talked in a language he hardly understood, while the other was the ship's photographer—a pale, limp man with the liquid eyes of a frightened deer. (John wondered what this man was doing in the middle of a war?)

His first angry impulse was to go to his brother and protest. Even if he was no longer a pilot why should he be ostracized this way? Wasn't there room for him somewhere with the men he had known and flown with? Why force him to live with these Stateside strangers whose duties he did not even understand?

But John hid his anger and shame as well as he could while he unpacked his gear and stowed it in the tiny space the other three a little grudgingly made for him.

As he stripped for a shower, one of the communicators looked up and saw the red and ugly scars streaming up his left arm and fanning out across his shoulder to die along his back.

"How'd you get in the Navy with an arm like that?" the man asked him.

John was sorry afterwards but at that instant he could not help it. He turned to the man and said, "I got that arm after I'd *been* in the Navy. If you're lucky you can get one too."

"That I can do without," the man said.

The photographer, his liquid eyes full of sympathy, said, "You've been in combat?"

John nodded as he got out a towel and wrapped it around his hips.

"What's it like?"

"Noisy," John said, pushing the dull-green curtain aside and leaving them.

However, as the days went by, John made friends with them. One he never really liked, but the other two, especially the photographer, he found to be interesting and worthwhile people.

The communicator he liked the best was named Hicks and was, John found out, an expert on radio. He spent a good deal of time building radio sets in the cabin, cluttering it up with wires and tubes and tools and stinking it up with the hot soldering iron, but in time John got interested in what he was doing, and Hicks encouraged him so that John even started building a circuit of his own.

But it was only a way to pass the endless time. At first he would go up on the flight deck to watch the take-offs and landings, but after awhile he stopped. The planes, the pilots, the flight deck crew and the hangar deck crew were in a different world, a different war. All he had to do battle with was a swirl of foolish paper.

Even in the wardroom he was left out. His seat at the dining table was between a communicator and a navigator—people who at least had something to *do*. All he could do was sit and listen to one talking about frequencies and the Fox schedule while the other talked about fixes and the Is-Was board.

The only thing he really accomplished was a letter to the Bureau of Medicine and Surgery, Navy Department, Washington 25, D.C., asking that the case of John Lawrence be reviewed and a waiver granted. The *Enterprise*'s doctor said he didn't think it would do any good but it wouldn't hurt to try. At least they'd give his wounded arm a re-examination and maybe he could pass it. (John made up his mind to and got ready for it. When none of his roommates were in the little cabin, he'd stand in front of the mirror and work that arm until at last, no matter how great the pain, he could keep it from showing in his face. He couldn't stop it from showing in his eyes, but he learned not to let the pain force him to draw a quick breath, or to wince, or tighten the muscles around his mouth. The docs would have to look pretty close to see it—and he hoped that they would not.)

4

The first amphibious invasion by U.S. troops since 1898 was made on the unknown island of Guadalcanal by 11,000 U. S. Marines on August 7, 1942.

It took the enemy forces on Guadalcanal totally by surprise, and the invasion troops were ashore by nightfall and by the next afternoon had captured the enemy's only airfield on the island.

It was quiet, uneventful movement of troops who met very little resistance from the enemy, but it was to generate a hurricane of war and a period of the most bitter, bloody and heroic combat ever endured by the United States Marine Corps.

For John Lawrence the invasion of Guadalcanal was the first step on a long and lonely journey—a journey on which he and his brother Jeff were to stake their lives.

PART THREE

THE ISLAND

1

From the air the island of Guadalcanal looked like a disease. The dark-green mat of the jungle had splotches of some sort of lighter green stuff—an ugly, crawling green— which looked like running sores. Hanging over the whole thing was a wispy vapor which writhed in long snake-like patterns and from the air looked as though it would smell bad.

John, in the back seat of the SBD, watched his brother's helmeted head as he leaned over to look down at this stinking island. "Looks like it's got leprosy," John said into the gosport.

"And everything else," Jeff said. "Buckle up, this landing's going to be rough."

Jeff brought the SBD around and lined her up with the airstrip first started by the Japanese and now being constantly worked on by the Navy's CBs and Marines. They had named it Henderson Field after a Marine aviator who had lost his life at the Battle of Midway, but as the SBD came lower, the "field" was a pretty ambitious word. The single strip whacked out of the jungle was pocked with bomb craters now full of water and was covered by a layer of thick mud. The Marine's Wildcat fighters were parked back in the jungle

which crowded right up to the edge of Henderson "Field,"
and as Jeff came in for the landing, the fighters looked as
though they had been put together with adhesive tape—or
chewing gum. John had never seen such a beat-up bunch of
airplanes.

John held the crate of spare radio parts firmly in his arms
as the SBD touched down between two bomb craters and
rolled forward, a plume of mud flying up behind and mud
beating a tattoo against the underside of the wings. And when
Jeff parked it, there was nothing to do but climb down into
the mud and slog through it to a tent back under some
ruined palm trees. Nailed to one of the trees was a crude sign
reading: OPERATIONS.

The men inside the tent startled John. They were bone-
thin and bone-tired and their sunken eyes looked out at you
as though you, too, were the enemy. Looking at them John
suddenly thought of The Survivor—he'd had this same terrible
look, this same thing about him that made you feel that he
was doomed. Just as these men in the tent were doomed—
and knew it.

John had gone through flight training with one of them, a
man named Hunter, who now greeted them and particularly
greeted with pleasure the spare parts John handed him.

"How's it going?" Jeff asked.

"Pretty good," Hunter said, gloating over the spare parts.

"Can the Marines hold the island?"

Hunter shrugged. "It's getting tougher every day. They
can throw anything they want in here and we can't stop 'em."

Another man said, "And not to mention Guadalcanal. You
spit-and-polish pilots don't know how good you've got it."
The man stood up and stared at John and Jeff, his eyes wild,
and in a moment his voice got wild too.

"Do you know that if you go to sleep on this island with-

out covering your whole face and head and neck with slimy
stinking mud, the mosquitoes will drain all the blood out of
you by morning? Did you know that?"

"And replace it with malaria," Hunter added.

"Did you know that if you want to wash that mud off,
you've got to fight your way through leeches who'll suck your
blood, too, and things in this Guadalcanal water that'll creep
inside you and kill you? Provided, of course, that the crocodiles don't eat you first."

The man held up one of his bare feet, and John saw for
the first time that it was rotting off.

"The Crud," the man said. "If you haven't got The Crud
on Guadalcanal you're not living right, brother. Bugs? You
want bugs? We got bugs. We got ticks—one bite, one boil.
We got a bug who'll get under your toenail and eat your foot
off before you can get to him. We got fleas, lice, bedbugs,
centipedes, spiders, ants, poisonous bees, scorpions—everything but good, harmless bugs."

The man sat down and stared at John. "You look healthy,"
he said. "Real healthy. *I* look healthy. I'm way ahead of these
other guys on Guadalcanal because all I've got is dysentery,
malaria and a touch of typhoid. But the rest of these jerks
have got gastroenteritis, yaws, elephantiasis, yellow fever,
scarlet fever, blackwater fever, bursitis, arthritis and a touch
of the old rheumatiz."

The man looked at John and laughed. "And they are also
insane."

"Well," Hunter said, "you wouldn't stay on Guadalcanal if
you had any sense."

The other man said, "Oh, I forgot to mention another
disease we have here on Guadalcanal. We have sniper bullets
through the head and also shrapnel through the lungs when
they bomb this field—which they do every night, Sundays in-

cluded—and, of course, we get shelled periodically from the sea. This kills a great many people." As he talked the man hobbled through the tent and, still talking, went outside.

"Don't mind him," Hunter said. "He got shot down yesterday."

"Sounds rough," John said.

"It *is* rough. They can come down The Slot with anything any time. They've got built-in surprise."

"Radar no good?" John asked.

"Not much," Hunter said, getting up. As he, too, hobbled over to the wall John noticed The Crud. "You see, they come down The Slot which protects them from radar. So we're just sitting ducks. Most of the time every plane we've got is sitting on the ground. If they're not, they still don't do much good because these old Wildcats have got to be on top to do any good. They can't be on the way up; they're too slow."

"What are they hitting you with?" Jeff asked.

"Those Val bombers, mostly. Of course they keep nuisance planes coming all the time. There's Washing Machine Charley who buzzes around dropping stuff all night—just to keep us awake. But the big stuff they deliver in the Vals. They're pretty good planes, Jeff. Lots of altitude and can travel. Without a lot of warning the Wildcats can't touch 'em. So—we're taking a beating. Every night we lose a couple of planes, the field gets bombed, and we get plastered—and I don't mean booze."

"Aren't you flying night searches?" Jeff asked.

"How can we? We haven't got planes enough, or gas enough or pilots who aren't too sick to fly a long search. We're trapped, Jeff. We've just got to sit here and let them come— there's nothing else we can do."

"This can't go on forever," Jeff said.

"No, it can't. And the Marines can't hold out forever,

either. I tell you, Jeff, we're holding the island with nothing but guts. The Marines are terrific, but how long can you ask a guy who's rotting to death to show a bit of the flag? Huh?"

"Suppose you had a two-hour warning that the Vals were on the way?" John asked.

Hunter turned around to stare at him with those deep, ruined eyes. "Two hours? Man, if we only had *half* an hour. If we *knew* when they were coming we could risk the planes and the gas and the pilots. We could get those old Wildcats up on the ceiling. . . ."

Hunter gazed out of the tent at the rain which had begun to fall. "Man," he said, in a low voice, "it would be a slaughter. Give us half an hour and we could murder 'em."

Then he turned back.

"But we don't get half an hour. We don't get sixty seconds. They get down behind those islands up The Slot, and the first we know is when we hear those bombs begin to whistle. You been up to the graveyard?"

John and Jeff stared at him.

"You ought to go," Hunter said. "One Marine up there must have been a poet. On his grave is a sign says:

> *And when he goes to Heaven*
> *To Saint Peter he will tell:*
> *Another Marine reporting, sir;*
> *I've served my time in Hell.*

A poet," Hunter said, looking out at the rain. "You'd better get out of here, Jeff. Before it gets so muddy you can't get out. And if you run across any admirals, tell 'em to send us planes and spare parts and gas and pilots who aren't half-dead. And anything else they can spare."

"They can't spare anything," Jeff told him.

"I know it. So if The Crud doesn't kill us the bombs will.

Come back some night and see how the other half lives—or dies. They're all around us in the jungle picking off anybody who moves. The Vals are dropping bombs on us and the ships are sitting out there shelling us point-blank."

John and Jeff told him good-by and then ran through the rain to the SBD, their feet sinking ankle-deep in the clinging mud.

It took full throttle to get the SBD moving, but at last Jeff lifted it off the bomb-scarred field and in a moment flew it out of the rain front and into the hot sunshine.

"Let's take a run up The Slot," John said, as Jeff flew out over Sealark Channel with Savo Island off to the left.

As Jeff banked the plane and settled on a course northward, John got out the chart and spread it on his knees. As the islands slipped below him, he checked them off—Santa Isabel, New Georgia, Kolombangara, Vella Lavella.

From 10,000 feet it was easy to see why they called it The Slot, for the islands lay in two parallel rows with the long channel of The Slot between them. Rows which went almost all the way to the great enemy base at Rabaul. Ships coming down The Slot bringing reinforcements to fight the Marines crawling through the jungle or to shell Henderson Field would be protected from the prying eye of radar by the rows of islands. Planes flying low over the channel would also be protected.

Radar couldn't find the enemy, John thought, but a man could.

"We'd better get out of here," Jeff said, "before we get jumped."

They were now over Choiseul—a big, gloomy island with rain clouds concealing the peaks of the mountains. As Jeff banked to turn back, John looked down at the island and the channel. The reefs made long white lines in the blue water and the jungle of the island was a dark, dark green.

Lying close to Choiseul and a little to the west of it was a small, green island with a bay marked by a curving sandy beach. There was no sign of houses or gardens on it—just a tiny, green island with the one curving beach.

"Let's go down and take a look," John suggested.

"A quick one," Jeff said, nosing the SBD down. "Might be guns over in the jungle here."

"Don't see any sign of any," John told him.

Jeff came in low from the channel and flew over the little island. Even from here there was no sign of man—no houses or boats or cleared places in the jungle.

"Paradise in the Pacific," Jeff said, looking down.

But John was interested in the island itself. He estimated that the highest part was at least five hundred feet above sea level. At 500 feet a man could see for twenty or thirty miles —almost all the way across The Slot.

He picked off the distance from Guadalcanal on the chart. Two hundred and ten miles. Those Val bombers, with non-retractable landing gear and a full load of bombs for the Marines, wouldn't make more than 150 miles an hour over the ground. It would take them an hour and twenty-five minutes to fly from this little island to Henderson Field.

An hour and twenty-five minutes.

"Going home," Jeff said, pulling up and away.

John swiveled the seat around and kept looking at the island as it fell away behind him. A channel which he estimated to be about a mile wide separated the little island from Choiseul, and directly across the channel he now saw a native village with the houses on stilts close to the beach and behind them little cleared places in the jungle. But he saw no sign of any enemy encampment.

An hour and twenty-five minutes. That, he thought, could be a long time.

He swiveled the seat around and looked at the back of his brother's head. There, he thought, is the only thing that can keep me out of this war. My brother.

2

It was time now to erase himself from the Navy, but as John sat on the edge of Hick's bed and tried to plan it, he discovered how many strings the Navy had tied to him. And he must cut them all without the men at the other end realizing that one lieutenant (j.g.) of the Naval Reserve was no longer on the end of them.

He found that it was almost easier to get killed.

He went to the paymaster. "I want to send all my pay home to my mother," John told him.

"*All* of it?" the officer asked, surprised.

"All of it."

"What are you going to use for money?"

"I'm a millionaire," John told him.

"Well, it takes all kinds to make a war. Now what's your mother's address?"

John told him and the officer wrote it down. "So I send your paychecks there every month, right?"

"Right."

Then John roamed around the ship until he found the Mess officer. "I won a little loot in a crap game," John told him. "So I'd better pay my mess bill while I can." He held out a wad of bills. "Four months in advance."

"In *advance*. Man, we could catch a bomb tomorrow and wipe out the whole affair."

"A bomb might ruin the flight deck and burn up the planes and stop the engines, but you'd still be charging us for chow. Four months in advance."

"Okay. But if that one with my number on it comes up I'm not going to give it back to you. Because I'll be too dead."

"Then you needn't worry about it," John told him.

"I probably won't."

Then he went to his cabin and began packing all his gear. When Hicks came in and saw him, he said, "Going on leave, Johnny?"

"Transferred. Since I'm no longer an aviator they're sending me over to the staff."

"VIP."

"Yeah, VIP. Very Ignorant Peon. I'll see you around."

John was sorry that he couldn't tell Hicks the truth but *all* of the Navy's strings must be cut, and that included the ones tying you to friends and shipmates.

He went to the Air Group Operations office. He waited until late at night to be sure that the yeoman wouldn't wander in. Locking the door just in case, he sat down at the typewriter and pecked out a set of orders transferring him to a ship whose name he made up. Putting the original in the To Be Burned bag, he filed the copy so that if he was missed, this would tell them where he was.

As he went about the ship steadily cutting himself loose from the Navy, his brother began to loom larger and larger as an obstacle. Jeff was the one man aboard this ship he couldn't lie to, nor play tricks on, nor confuse with fake orders. Jeff was not only his brother, but his commanding officer. You might get away with losing yourself with the paymaster and the Mess officer but what could you do to erase yourself from the ranks of your commanding officer?

John decided that he would come to that only after he had

done everything that needed to be done. Then he'd present it to Jeff.

He went up through the island to the navigator's and checked tides, currents, phase of the moon and the movements of the sun. He jotted them down, noting particularly that the moon would rise tomorrow night at 8:45 and the tide would be high at 9:10.

He went into the meteorological shack and got the forecast; clear sky except for widely scattered rain squalls; wind west at three to four knots. But within five days, the forecast was for rain.

Next he went to the Gunnery officer, who at first refused to issue him one of the Smith & Wesson .38-caliber revolvers. "They're for pilots only, Johnny."

John told him: "The only way I can get a medal now is shoot expert pistol. Don't you want me to have a medal?"

"You already got a Navy Cross," the Gunnery officer argued. "And a Purple Heart."

"I don't want to look like a hero," John said, "So give me a gun and let me practice."

He got a gun, a hundred rounds of ammunition and a shoulder holster. As he signed for them the Gunnery officer said, "It's funny how hard it is for a guy to get a gun, and here we are in the middle of a war."

He stopped in a vacant corridor only dimly lit by the blue battle lights and rooted around in his Valpack until he found a set of wings. He pinned them onto his shirt which was now soaking with sweat in the terrible heat of the closed and darkened ship. Then as he went down the steep ladders, he hoped that the parachute riggers on duty tonight wouldn't recognize him. That they wouldn't be the same ones who used to pack his chute before Midway.

And they were not. As he went into the long, hot room

with the long, long, glass-smooth table, the three riggers working on a chute were strangers to him. The white chute was stretched down the length of the table, and the men were carefully folding it in and at the same time arranging the spreaders in orderly loops.

"If that one's for me," John said, "don't goof it, please."

"Never had any complaints," a rigger said. "Nobody ever brought one back and said it wouldn't open."

"Just too embarrassed, that's all."

He stood and watched them as they finished packing the chute. Leaning against the bulkhead, watching, he thought how much he would miss them—all of them, everyone in the ship. They were such good people. Like the riggers down in this hot, stinking room folding that chute as though they themselves were going to jump it. Good people. He would miss them.

This was his lucky night. He met no one he knew all the way from the parachute riggers to the flight deck. In the darkness there he couldn't be recognized as he walked over to Jeff's plane and hid the chute in the gunner's seat.

For fifteen minutes he walked up and down the dark, windswept flight deck trying to figure a way to get binoculars. Binoculars were almost as hard to get as a trip home. Of course, he could sneak into the admiral's stateroom and steal his stars and . . . but whoever saw a twenty-three-year-old admiral? Could he claim he was the new navigator? Hardly. His seat in the wardroom was next to one of the navigators.

Going back into the heat and stink of the island, he climbed up inside it to the bridge.

It was almost silent on the bridge now. The lights were so dimmed that people were only outlines against the sky. The light from the compass shone a little on the helmsman's intent face, a few dim red and green warning lights glowed on the board, but that was all.

The people were still and intent, the captain sitting in the high swivel chair staring straight forward at the sea. The helmsman stood at the wheel, only his arms moving a little as he held the ship on course. The rest of the dim figures stood, facing forward, silent, waiting.

The Officer of the Deck walked over to John's side of the bridge and looked at the Night Order Book, holding it down low so he could read it. He then gave a quiet order to change course as he zigzagged the *Enterprise* so that an enemy submarine couldn't hold a steady bearing on it. Around the OD's neck was a leather strap and to this was attached the long 7×50 Navy binoculars.

A mess boy came onto the bridge then with a little tray, a somewhat battered but shiny metal coffee pot and two cups. He poured the captain a cup and then another for the Officer of the Deck.

John had been waiting, pressed back into the darkness, for exactly this.

The Officer of the Deck pulled the leather strap of his binoculars up over his head, wrapped it around the glasses and set them down on the chart table. Then he went over and took his cup of coffee. As they drank, he and the captain talked almost in whispers.

No one seemed to be looking in his direction as John stepped forward in the darkness, picked up the binoculars and stepped back to the door of the bridge.

But, as he opened the door, he heard the orderly say in a surprised tone, "Hey, those are the OD's!"

John slipped out of the door, closed it behind him and then moved over into the deeper darkness in a corner of the bridge structure.

In a moment the door opened and the orderly hurried out, saying to no one, "Hey. Come back with the glasses!"

John watched him go on down the ladder, and when he was out of sight he turned, crossed to the other side, and went fast down the ladder, stuffing the binoculars inside his shirt as he hurried.

It was his lucky night. He reached the flight deck without seeing anyone and once out there in the windy darkness, he was safe. Pretending to be out for only a breath of air he wandered aft to the planes spotted for the morning Combat Air Patrol. He disappeared among them and without being seen, got up on the wing of Jeff's plane and hid the binoculars under the seat.

So maybe he'd go to jail. Could that be any worse than Guadalcanal?

The rest was easy—the kr   Mae West with all the survival gear, some atabrine p   m sickbay (he just walked in and took them), a new pair of flight deck boots.

And now there was only his brother standing like a wall between him and what he wanted to do.

It was two in the morning when he knocked on the door of Jeff's stateroom. As he went in it seemed to him that Jeff looked a little guilty or furtive about something, but then he thought that was probably his own guilt.

Jeff had been working at the little metal desk and when he saw his brother, stood up, his back to the desk. With his hands behind him he closed a book he had been reading. The whole gesture was as though he did not want John to see the book.

Jeff's roommate was asleep in the other bunk, the fan blowing across him but not cooling him as the air was hot and heavy.

"Are you awake or walking in your sleep?" Jeff asked.

John put his hands out in front of him in the manner of a sleepwalker. "Come on in, the dreams are fine," he said, almost in a whisper so as not to wake up the sleeping man. "Ever change the air in here?"

"Can't afford to. You see, when this war is over I'm going to sell this stuff for souvenirs."

"Want to try the stuff they've got topside?" John asked, and waited. If Jeff didn't want to go out into the privacy of the flight deck all of his plans and schemes and preparations would be lost. (And how, he wondered, could he put those binoculars back?)

"Wait," Jeff said. "I'll get my gas mask so I won't have to breathe any of that fresh air."

They left the cabin quietly and didn't talk as they went through the dimly lit a inking ship and out onto the flight deck.

There was moonlight ng and going as the broken clouds drifted across the sky. The ship's speed plus the wind's threw a blast of cool, fresh air down the long gray expanse of the deck and whistled around the dark planes standing ready on the stern, their wings folded up. To John the planes looked asleep. But not soundly. Tensely and nervously asleep, waiting only to wake up and start their dry roaring.

The brothers walked forward, leaning against the wind until they came to the bow of the ship. Looking down they watched the black Pacific flowing toward the prow and a it reached the cutwater, breaking into two smooth, flowing, white bodies of water which, while varying in size and shape and whiteness, never stopped forming and flowing aft.

"This is no night to be on Guadalcanal," Jeff said.

John had been waiting for an opening so that he could start the speeches he had thought out and almost memorized. The reasons for what he wanted to do. The value of it. The necessity. The lives it would save. He had it ready to say if only Jeff would listen.

They turned and started aft, walking much faster now with the wind pounding against their backs.

"Night like this," Jeff went on, "and those Val bombers couldn't miss. You know, I didn't recognize Hunter at first. When I saw him in Pearl three months ago he was fat, dumb and happy."

"Jeff, did you know that there was a radio transmitter now that doesn't weigh but about fifty pounds, motor generator and all?"

Jeff said, "That so?" And then he went on, "If the Nips throw us off Guadalcanal it's going to add years to this war."

John said, "With a transmitter like that a man could keep in touch."

Jeff said, "I don't see how the Marines can stand it. I heard about one Marine who didn't get a chance to take his shoes off for twenty days. And when he finally got them off— no feet."

John said, "They've got one of them aboard ship."

"One of what? The Marine's feet?"

"No. One of those transmitters I was talking about."

"Oh? But what I was saying—suppose they push us off Guadal? It'd not only be a defeat but. . . ."

John interrupted him. "So why not do something about it?"

Jeff stopped on the flight deck and looked at him. "Do something?" he asked quietly.

"Not you," John said. "Me. I can do something. Not much, but something."

A cloud moved out from under the moon and the brothers stood there in the soft, shadowless light and looked at each other.

"Are you thinking about that island, Johnny?"

Jeff had always been like this, John thought, relief almost making him laugh.

"Yeah, that island," John said. "Drop me and one of those transmitters . . . and a good pair of binoculars which I happen to have. . . ."

"So it was you who stole the OD's glasses." Jeff began to laugh and they walked on down the deck, laughing.

"I've been thinking about it, Johnny. Getting you on that enemy island with a radio isn't half as hard as getting you away from the U. S. Navy."

"I've already done it," John said, and told him how.

Jeff stopped and laughed again. "Ever since I saw Hunter and the rest of them in that tent I've been wondering how we could help them. How to give them that half-hour warning they need. You must have been thinking the same thing."

"And wondering how I could persuade you to do it. Because nobody else can take me up there," John said. "They'd be afraid to."

Jeff walked all the way to the parked planes before he asked quietly, "Aren't you afraid, Johnny?"

"Scared stiff. But look, Jeff, what good am I doing? I came out here to fly planes and drop bombs and sink ships. I didn't come to push papers from an In to an Out basket. I'm expendable," he said, and laughed.

"We all are, I guess. But you never think of it as just one. I mean you, yourself, getting it. It's always, well, a bunch of guys get it like Torpedo Eight. And you go with them."

"I'd rather be sitting on a beautiful, tropical island than on that hard parachute in an airplane that smells like castor oil and a few other things. Why defy gravity?"

"One thing bothers me," Jeff said. "I've been reading the secret reports on what the Australians call coast watchers.

Civilians, mostly—a sort of underground outfit. They're catching it. And the worst part of it is that the natives are the ones who're turning them over to the Japs. Natives that these guys have known for years. Not because they're unfriendly. Because the Japs threaten to kill them, and their wives and children, if they don't squeal on the coast watchers."

"In other words," John said, "I can have the bending palms but keep away from those natives."

"Something like that. Because if you get on that island you're going to be all by yourself, John. There isn't even going to be a Torpedo Eight to go along with you. Have you thought of that?"

"So I'm by myself. Look, you go out with a squadron of planes—like VT-8—and your number comes up. Do you go with a bunch of guys? You do not. In the last seconds you're just as all by yourself as I'll be on that island. So let's stop yakking about the Great Beyond and get under way. You take me up there tomorrow night—" John paused and looked at the glow of sunrise on the horizon. "*Tonight.* I'll take along all I can carry. Then tomorrow night, you come back with the radio and the rest of the stuff. If everything goes all right I should be running a broadcasting station from that island in twenty-four hours. I figure I can see any planes coming down The Slot and most of the ships. If the guys on Guadalcanal get on the ball they'll have at least an hour's warning. That'll give 'em plenty of time to get those old Wildcats up and parked at 30,000 feet. It'll be a turkey shoot."

"It'll be lonely," Jeff said. "For you."

"If you don't think it's lonely here, get yourself grounded and go up in the ready room where you used to be a plane driver. I'll take that island any time. So let's go."

The sun was coming up now but they walked on, up and down the flight deck, pushing forward against the wind, almost being blown aft by it.

They planned and worked out the problems and lined up the details.

Careful plans, and good ones, but the brothers did not know one thing. And this they would find out in time.

3

It was dusk when the brothers came out on the flight deck. As planned, they came from different directions and reached the SBD separately, Jeff getting there first. He stopped on the starboard side of the plane and instead of climbing on up on the wing, he stopped and discussed the cowl vents with the plane captain and was assured that the vents were opening all the way now and that he would have no more trouble with them.

And as they stood on the flight deck and talked, John, moving in the semi-gloom of dusk, approached the plane from the starboard side, climbed quickly up into the gunner's seat and once there, strapped on his chute and harness and slumped down in the seat, his flight helmet on, his goggles pulled down.

Now Jeff and the plane captain got up on the wing. The captain helped Jeff into his cockpit, checked his harness and chute and then leaned back toward John.

John pretended to be doing something on the other side of the plane as the captain said, "You okay, Guns?"

"Okay," John said.

He found that his breath was shivering as the plane captain got down off the wing and Jeff started the engine. The plane captain was his last link with the Navy, and as Jeff turned up the engine, John was sure that he had not been recognized.

It made him feel a little lost to know that now no one on this ship; no one in the huge bureaus of the Navy, no friend, no shipmate knew where he was nor where he was going. No one would miss him, no one would search for him. As far as the Navy was concerned, John Lawrence, Lieutenant (j.g.) U. S. Naval Reserve, did not now exist. . . .

It was good to fly with a man like Jeff. As he took off into the darkness of the approaching night, John looked out of the plane, watching the flight deck streaming out from under him, faster and faster. He looked at the dim figures of the deck crew and watched the men running to their battle stations for evening G.Q. He looked up at the island where the shadowy men stood, conning this ship through these waters which belonged now to the enemy. (He hoped that the Officer of the Deck would forgive him for making off with the binoculars. I need them worse than you do, John said to himself. And you can get brand-new ones.)

He saw the long black muzzles of the antiaircraft guns swinging up toward the night sky. He saw a gunner sitting in the bucket seat playing soundlessly on a harmonica. He saw Lieutenant Conklin, the Signal officer, come out on the deck and relish the cool of night and the ending of the burning sun on his red and tender skin.

They passed over where the ready room was and John thought of the pilots there. Sleeping in the big chairs, yakking about home and girls, playing poker for a month's pay a card (what difference did it make when this might be your last pay check in this life?). He wondered what the New York banker was doing? And Hicks. Was Hicks getting that radio ready—wrapping it in rubber sheeting and waterproofing it. Getting it all ready, he had been told, to be delivered to the Marines on Guadalcanal.

John wondered, as the plane swept on toward the forward end of the ship, what it felt like to be one of the black gang down in the bowels of the *Enterprise*. Especially during a fight. They couldn't know what was going on around the flight deck. Couldn't know what enemy plane might be diving now, right now, down on the ship to drop its bomb down and down through the decks. Couldn't know what submarine was lying waiting with all tubes manned and ready. What was it like for the black gang he wondered? To be sitting down in the engine rooms writing a letter home, or drinking thick coffee out of the thick, forever stained old Navy mugs, or checking the dials and valves and hearing the enunciator clanging away for a change of rpm—what would it be like then to have the torpedo come into the compartment where you were? Like nothing, probably. Just one minute you're writing a letter to your kid at home, keeping the words short and simple so he'll understand, and the next minute you and your letter aren't there any more. You just aren't there. That's all.

Jeff made his usually sure, easy, floating take off. Jeff never horsed a plane, nor faltered. He was so completely competent and under such complete control that the plane always moved in *flight*.

John swiveled the seat around so that he was facing aft and looked back at the *Enterprise*.

And saw it vanish, engulfed by the darkness. One second the ship was there, in the next it was gone.

He wondered if he would ever see it again.

And he had forgotten to bring a toothbrush. He patted the pockets on the legs of his flight suit—no toothbrush. And on the corner of the island he was going to, there wasn't goin to be any drug store.

"I left my toothbrush," he said to Jeff.

"Well now, that's a real tragedy," Jeff told him. "But I'll drop you one tomorrow. What color do you like?"

"Don't bother, I'll just run downtown and get one."

"You got that gun?" Jeff asked seriously.

John patted the gun in the shoulder holster and patted the heavy bulge in the pocket on his right thigh. "Yeah."

He wanted to go on talking but there was nothing to talk about. Already he was slipping out of the world he had known; already his mind and his soul (he guessed) had gone on ahead to that island, leaving only his body now strung with gadgets sitting in the plane.

After awhile Jeff said, "Iron Bottom Bay."

John looked down through the thousands of feet of night toward the dark sea and the dark islands below. Only by the reefs and beaches showing up ghostly against the black sea could he tell that Savo Island and Guadalcanal and Tulagi lay below him. There was not a glimmer of light anywhere on Guadal, and the diseased patches were now only faint marks on the darkness of the jungle.

But there were thousands of Marines down there in that darkness, lying in that jungle, waiting out the long night; waiting for that terrible, feminine whine of the sniper rifles. Marines who figured that if you heard it, good. You were alive.

They were down there, Hunter and the rest with The Crud and the afflictions and the useless radar. Just lying there in the mud with their faces an inch thick with mud, listening and waiting for the high, hard hammering of the Vals coming in on them. Or the crump of the shells from the ships that they didn't even know had steamed into Iron

and were sitting there offshore, firing into the
̄en had been sleeping or lobbing explosives onto
̄ield and thus ruining it for take-off, even though
wobbling pilots slogged through the mud to
their planes and tried to get them off the ground. Too late,
too late.

Jeff flew steadily at 10,000 feet. Below them The Slot slid
slowly by, marked by the dark blotches of the islands.

"You getting ready?" Jeff asked after awhile.

"I'm about as ready as I'll ever be. Which isn't very ready.
I wish I'd taken 'em up on that voluntary jump at Pensacola.
Wonder what it's like?"

"I do, too. But guys do it all the time so it must be pretty
simple. Just go 'One—Missouri—two—Missouri—' until you
get to ten and pull the red handle and you're in business."

"Did you hear about that Marine aviator who pulled the
red handle and nothing happened? So he fell 2000 feet into
the sea and all he did was break his legs?"

"Must have wanted to get down in a hurry. I'll take the
slow road."

"Must have. Hope the moon doesn't goof up and forget
it's due to shine tonight."

"If it doesn't come up in fifteen minutes we'll send out a
complaint."

But the moon came up on time and was exactly the shape
the meteorologist had predicted it would be. Very smart
meteorologist, John thought. Very smart man.

"Going down," Jeff said. "Ladies lingerie, toys, apes, coconuts and bending palms."

He nosed the SBD down and watched the altimeter needle
unwind. At 5000 feet he leveled off.

Choiseul lay just ahead of them now, and John's little

island shone in the new moonlight, its curving beach as white as a bone in the sun.

"Johnny," Jeff said quietly, "I've been thinking."

John knew he couldn't stand much of that. "Don't," he said, almost angrily.

"We can turn around now and forget the whole thing. I can even get those binoculars back to the OD."

"Mustn't waste the Navy's gas just sight-seeing," John told him.

But he was afraid now. Up until right now he had not been really afraid. He had had too much to think about, too many plans to make and binoculars to steal. But now all that was behind him, vanished like the *Enterprise*. Ahead of him was the jump, and the island and the dangerous loneliness; the unknown.

The jump. It was so far, so dark. So far—falling through all that darkness.

He looked down at the island and thought of himself—his body itself—falling all that way.

John suddenly remembered the rubber boat. Lifting his feet and getting his legs out of the way, he hauled the deflated boat up from the floor of the cockpit. Then holding it against the slipstream, he leaned out and looked down.

It was *now*. He dropped the boat and watched it go tumbling down through the sky, a dark, rectangular bundle which soon disappeared into the darkness of the night and the jungle below so that he could not see where it landed.

"I dropped the boat, but couldn't see where it landed. On the island somewhere."

Jeff laughed a little. "You'll have plenty of time to find it."

John started to say, "Maybe the rest of my life . . ." but he didn't.

"The wind's about five knots from due west," Jeff said, his

voice suddenly sounding far away and impersonal. Like the voices on the loud-speakers at airports, John thought. "If you start over the channel you should clear the island and land in that little bay. It'll be to leeward so the water'll be calm. Nothing like a swim in the moonlight for the spirits."

John looked down at his gloved hands lying motionless in his lap. All I've got to do, he said to himself, is to leave them right there. That's all. Just leave them. Don't move them.

But his right hand came up slowly and touched the quick release on the shoulder harness. John felt the harness' pressure slack off even though the wide, webbed straps still rested on his shoulders and the buckle shone prettily in the moonlight.

His hand moved down and pulled the quick release on the safety belt and that, too, released him from its embracing pressure.

Then with both hands he pulled the chute harness up as tight as it would go.

And then there was nothing more to do but—get out.

Now is the time, John thought, for that epic wisecrack. Like in the movies just before the hero dies (but he's not really going to die) he says this really wild remark that makes you choke up and cry he's so brave.

"I'm ready," was all he could say.

Jeff banked the plane smoothly and then leveled off again. "I'll fly the upwind leg and give you the word, John."

"Okay."

"When you go, give a good shove so you'll clear the tail, hear?"

"Yeah."

"And they tell me that you've got lots of time to take that ten count. But if you rush it you're in trouble."

"Yeah. One—Missouri. . . ."

"Johnny?" Jeff said.

"Johnny, aye, aye."

"You remember that thing in the Bible or somewhere that says 'No greater love hath any man. . . .' Or something like that."

"Yeah, I remember it."

"Well, okay. I guess I know how you feel and you know how I feel."

"Yeah," John said. The fear was making him sick. The way he was the night before Midway. It was so dark, so far.

"I'll be back tomorrow night at ten sharp with the radio and the rest of the gear. Am I right now?: one fire on the beach if you're okay. Two if you can't swing it and want a submarine or something to come take you off. Right?"

"That's right. Two if in trouble. But not big fires they can see all over the place. So look hard."

"I will. Now look, I'll drop the gear at fifty feet and hope it comes down near the beach. If it lands in the sea though, it'll float. But you'd better be ready to swim for it. That's a pretty narrow beach."

"I'll be ready."

John pushed himself up out of the seat. Unzipping the front of his flight suit, he put the binoculars with the lenses taped up inside and used the wrist strap to secure them so they wouldn't beat him to death on the way down Now, half-standing up in the cockpit, he said, "Okay, Jeff. Say the word." He could see Jeff looking alternately down at the island and then at his instruments.

"Have a good trip and come back soon," Jeff said.

"X marks the spot—wish you were here."

They both laughed and were both surprised. But it didn't last.

"Fifteen seconds, Johnny."

John put his hand up to the microphone cord. When he pulled it that would be the end of words.

"So long, Jeff," he said, his hand on the cord.

"So long, Johnny. Good luck."

John pulled the cord and let it drop. Then he pushed himself upright against the slipstream blast, got a foot up into the seat. Then a leg over.

The sudden blast struck him and almost hurled him out and back. His feet skidded on the side of the plane as he tried to push clear of it and for a moment he felt himself sliding back along the fuselage.

And then he fell clear as the tail surfaces of the plane slammed past him, blotting out the moon for a split second.

The knowledge that he was falling came slowly. He had been so frightened by the threat of being struck by the tail of the plane, that he was still concerned with it now that he was far below Jeff and the SBD and was tumbling, turning over and over slowly, through the air.

It was soft and warm and he did not seem to be going very fast. He was lying on his back now, looking up at the moonlit sky, then at the moon itself as it swung crazily around. He looked for the plane but could not find it and felt bitterly abandoned by his brother. And then the land and the sea swung around and came closer.

In a sudden panic he began to count. Both of his hands, as though belonging to someone else, started a frantic search for the ripcord ring.

He was counting much too fast and could not remember how far he had gotten, nor guess at how many seconds he had been falling.

And now he could no longer judge, for the land and sea had disappeared and the sky and moon were the only things he could see.

John twisted around in the air and looked down. The island was rushing up toward him with horrible speed.

"Six—Missouri—seven—Missouri—"

His voice sounded oddly loud and clear.

"Eight—Missouri—nine . . ."

His right hand had the ring now. "Don't toy with it," he remembered an instructor saying. "Pull it! Give it all you've got because that's the only way you'll get it open."

". . . Missouri . . ."

His gloved fingers clamped hard around the metal ring protruding a little way from the canvas pocket it rested in.

He was surprised to hear someone shout "ten!" and then recognized his own voice.

John pulled the ring. For a second it slid smoothly out of the pocket and then without warning, it stopped moving, jammed.

"Pull it!" the instructor had said, ". . . because that's the only way you're going to get it open."

He pulled again with the strength of panic.

He felt something give way, break, and then there was no more resistance. He might as well have been pulling air.

He was now lying face skyward, his legs sprawled out, his left arm dangling. He was slowly revolving backward but now the moon was full on him.

There in his gloved hand was the metal ring and dangling from it, was a two-foot length of thin stainless steel cable. At the end of the cable there was *nothing*. It was just a broken length of steel cable dangling in the moonlight.

In sick fear John moved his hand away from his body and let the ring and the broken cable drop. There was now nothing he could do but wait out the seconds until this free-falling through the sky would end either in the black sea, or the black jungle. What difference did it make, he wondered. And decided that it made no difference at all.

He had fallen backward so that now he was upside down, his head plunging toward the sea, his feet waving in the sky. The wind around him whistled sharply, but through that sound he could hear the sound of the SBD's engine. It was flat and far away and directionless. It was, John decided, on the way home.

Jeff had abandoned him, he thought, with a bitterness like fire in his throat. Just gone off and left him without even waiting to see if the chute was going to open.

As the sound of the plane faded away, a new sound took its place and John listened to it, wondering what it was, where it came from? Perhaps, he thought, the sea? Washing on the beach. Swish, swish, swish.

It reminded him of the times at night when he was only a baby when his mother would come into his room. It would be dark and still and silent in there, and then there would be the warm, nice, comforting sound of his mother, the silk she wore making a sound like this as she moved toward his bed. Swish, swish, swish.

Now he was face down, looking with bleak eyes at the black jungle of the island rushing up toward him. He was lying there in the sky, sprawled out, helpless . . . and then it hit him. At one moment he was lying there, swiftly falling with the swishing sound close beside him. In the next something slammed him to a stop, jerked him painfully around and then dropped a crushing weight on him.

He thought for a moment that he had hit the island or the sea, but he was still in the air and still falling.

But slowly now; floating, really.

He was afraid to raise his head and look up for fear that he would see nothing but the sky and the clouds and the moon. He knew that he had broken the chute—he had seen the broken cable dangling from the ring in his hand.

But he *had* to look up.

The moon shone beautifully through the great, white, shining umbrella of silk swaying gently to and fro above him.

Now he was truly floating—fine feeling of freedom. He looked down and saw the little island moving slowly past him, his feet dangling across it and swaying a little.

And he could hear things now. The hard whistling of the wind had stopped, and there were soft sounds of the sea against the land, the faint sighing of the wind in the shrouds of the chute and suddenly growing louder, the sound of a plane engine.

John looked all around for it and suddenly saw the SBD wheeling down toward him.

It almost made him cry to see his brother sitting there in the plane, circling in the night, watching him. Now he waved a gloved hand, and in the moonlight, John could see him smiling.

The SBD followed him down as far as it could and then circled slowly as John went the rest of the way.

Suddenly, as he fell, his speed grew much greater; at least it seemed to him to be greater. Now the dark mass of the jungle swept past him, the little beach of the island suddenly appeared white and smooth, and then it, too, swept past him and he was out over the water.

When he struck the sea it knocked the wind out of him. He hadn't expected to hit so hard; to end that beautiful, floating sensation with this abrupt and banging descent into the water.

For a long moment he thought he was going to be drowned in the tangle of ropes pulling at him, pulling him through and under the water, but at last he got free of the chute harness and the tangled shrouds and found the lanyards on the CO_2 bottles.

The bottles went off with a loud hissing and the yellow Mae West life jacket suddenly expanded all around him, lifting his head out of the water and making him feel light and supported.

Now he looked around. The white blotch of the chute was still visible but it was sinking fast. Above him Jeff was still circling low over the water. To his left was his island.

Somehow, as he looked at the island, it no longer seemed to be a green and pretty place—a little paradise in the Pacific. For it was now dark and gloomy and somehow menacing with its mass of dark and solid jungle outlined by the stark trunks of the palm trees which grew along the shore.

John started swimming toward it. With all the gear he had tied to him and loading down his pockets, he was slow and awkward in the water and the Mae West was a bulky arrangement, but finally he could touch bottom. In a moment he was wading steadily out of the water, the white beach almost shining ahead of him.

He stopped then and waved with both arms to his brother still circling above him and saw Jeff wave back, and then the SBD turned and began to climb. John stood waist-deep in the water watching it go, watching until it disappeared into the darkness leaving only a faint flickering of orange color from the exhaust stacks, and then they were gone, too.

But he would be back tomorrow night, John told himself. Back with the radio and food. And then when he got the radio going, it would be easy. Whenever he needed anything he could call up the Marines on Guadalcanal, and they could get the message out to Jeff on the *Enterprise*.

John felt less lonely as he waded on toward the beach. He

wasn't completely cut off from the world he had just left. As long as Jeff was around he'd be all right.

And if this little island turned out to be so dangerous that he could not stay on it, as soon as Jeff brought the radio, he could yell for help, and a sub or one of the PT boats at Tulagi could come tearing up The Slot on a dark night and rescue him.

Everything was going to be all right, John argued.

He was about to step out on the sand of the beach when he suddenly realized that from now on he had better start being careful. Footprints on a beach on an island where no man was wouldn't look good to an enemy patrol.

Wading in foot-deep water, he went the length of the beach and then on through some tangled, tough-branched bushes which grew not only down to the water but out into it. He shoved his way into them for a few feet and then turned and fought his way over to the island itself. Soon he was under the palm trees and could walk freely.

The ground beneath the tall palms was almost bare of growing things but littered with the debris from the palms themselves. The dried, broken fronds from the trees lay everywhere, and under his feet he felt the shape of coconuts. Beyond the palms, however, the jungle looked impenetrable —a wall of growing stuff, now menacing in the darkness.

In a little cleared area he stopped, took off the Mae West and deflated it. Then he untied the OD's binoculars from around his chest and put them on the Mae West. Next he took off the shoulder holster and now could skin out of the wet flight suit. Under this he was wearing uniform trousers and shirt with his lieutenant's insignia and on the left breast, his tarnished gold wings. He skinned these off, too, and was shocked to see how white his underwear was. That was a detail he had not thought of: he should have dyed them some dark color. He made a mental note to get the word to Jeff to drop him some dark-colored clothing.

He wrung out all his clothes and laid them out on the palm fronds. His tanned, naked body was a good deal less visible than the glaring white skivvies. He put the holster back on and then went carefully down the beach, keeping back in the dark shadows.

There was no sign of habitation. No houses, no boats or campsites. He could not be sure about footprints on the sandy beach.

When he got to the end of the island, he could see across the channel to Choiseul. The high mountains were capped with banks of cloud from which the dark jungle streamed like a blanket. But on the beach where the natives lived there were pinpoints of light which from the yellow color and flickering he decided must be open fires or perhaps some sort of open oil lamps such as Eskimos use. For a moment the sight of the little flickering lights made him feel good, until he remembered Jeff talking about the Australian coast watchers who had been betrayed to the enemy by the natives.

He suddenly thought of his watch and in quick panic raised his arm to his ear and listened. The tick was faint but steady, and in the darkness he saw that it was almost midnight.

Tomorrow, he decided, was the time to go on exploring. He turned back and still keeping in the shadows, found his clothes.

For a while he sat with his back against one of the palms and fought off loneliness and a feeling of defeat—the old feeling of knowing that something was going to go wrong and that he was going to goof again. Something that was not his fault, not his error or mistake. An Act of God.

He ached all over from the jerk of the chute and the landing and he was both hungry and thirsty, but there was nothing to eat. He got up, got the knife out of the Mae West, and hacked for a while at a coconut but couldn't get it open. In the morning, he decided.

Everything was going to be all right tomorrow. Tomorrow there would be food and a stove and above all, the radio. By this time tomorrow night, he figured, he would be talking to the Marine radio on Guadalcanal. That would be good.

He put the wet, cold flight suit back on and then to protect his feet, he put on his heavy, wet socks.

The mosquitoes had found him now so he put the helmet on, too, strapping it under his chin. Then his gloves. Now all that the mosquitoes could get to was his face.

On Guadalcanal tonight, a thousand Marines were coated with mud. John dug down through layers of dead stuff until he got to the earth which was dank and gummy. He smeared the nasty smelling stuff all over his face and then put his goggles on to protect the area around his eyes.

Ready at last for bed, he sat down with his back against the tree, took the .38 out of the holster, put it in his lap and tried to sleep.

He must have slept a little, for sometime in the night a sound woke him up. At first he thought it was planes, but as it came slowly closer he knew that it could not be.

He went over to the Mae West, got the binoculars, peeled the tape off the lenses and held them up to the moon. Very good glasses, he decided. They had not been damaged at all by the jump or the landing, or even the immersion in sea water.

Going down to the edge of the palms but not out into the moonlight, he trained the glasses out over The Slot.

There she was. A ship streaming down from the north. Not very big and not very fast. A coastal freighter.

She was about a mile out from his island and moving at not more than ten knots. There were no lights visible, but he could clearly hear the slow throb of her engines.

Now if this were only tomorrow night, he thought, I could be talking to the Marines right now, telling them that a small freighter was coming down The Slot toward them.

But all he could do now was to brace himself against a tree trunk and watch.

He expected the ship to continue on course and fade away into the darkness, but it did not. About a mile south of his island, the ship made a full ninety-degree turn and moved toward Choiseul.

Somehow this was alarming. John got up and went down the length of his island so that from the southern tip, he could see the ship again.

She turned once more, this time ninety degrees to the north, and steamed straight up the channel between his island and the mainland of Choiseul.

She was not more than a quarter of a mile away now, and he could even see figures of men moving about on the deck and the faint glow of light coming from the pilot house.

And in a moment she stopped, and John clearly heard the anchor splash into the water and then the chain running out through the hawse holes.

And now, on the deck there were dozens, perhaps hundreds of men.

With fear growing in him like some sort of uncontrollable fungus, John sat with his back against a tree and watched.

After the loading booms were rigged out, they lowered what John took to be a lighter or big barge down into the water. Onto this they swung the cargo net filled with crates, boxes and barrels of various sizes. Men streamed down landing nets onto the barge and stacked the stuff as it was lowered to them.

That this was the enemy John had no doubt, and that he had come to this place to stay was becoming more and more evident.

Now over the side of the ship they lowered a motorboat John figured was about thirty-feet long. A crew scrambled down into it, and soon he heard the motor start.

Within an hour the barge was stacked high with gear and the motorboat, running back and forth between the ship and Choiseul, had landed what John estimated to be at least fifty men. Soldiers or Marines, for they were equipped with enormous packs, small arms and rifles.

Just before dawn they cast off the lines on the barge, and the motorboat towed it slowly over to the beach. There the troops unloaded it like a horde of hungry ants and within half an hour, the barge was being lifted back aboard the ship.

They did not, however, lift the motorboat back aboard. John saw them moor that close along the beach.

Again he heard anchor chain rattling, and as the sun began to come up, the ship steamed away along the channel, going north.

Over on the beach there was a jumble of crated gear, barrels, boxes and bundles.

And at least fifty armed men who now in the early sunlight moved almost frantically around. A large group of them were digging furiously, their shovel blades flashing in the light, the earth flying. Others were on the beach shoveling sand into bags which still others carried up to where the men were digging.

For a long time as John sat there watching, he couldn't figure out what they were doing, but when they apparently had dug their hole deep enough and sandbagged it well enough, it became sickeningly clear what they were doing.

The gun was a long-barreled, wicked-looking thing. It took all of the men to drag it over and lower it down into the sandbagged hole.

With the gun in place, the men formed a long line and passed ammunition; round after round of it, the copper cases glowing in the sunlight.

While the ammunition was being passed into the hole, other men had been going back and forth from the jungle to the gun, each one carrying a branch, or a log or fronds.

John, sick with fear now, kept on watching as the enemy slowly vanished into the green jungle. They camouflaged the gun pit with leaves and limbs (but the gun could appear with startling speed). The rest of the supplies they stacked well back in the jungle and covered with vines and tarpaulins.

Even their tents vanished. John would watch two men erect a tent, clearing away the jungle only enough to get a tent up, but when they finished the greenish-gray cloth of the tents melted into the color of the jungle.

Even the uniforms they wore were greenish, and their dark yellow faces seemed part of the camouflage.

They even made the boat vanish. They pulled it in close to the shore and spread coconut fronds and vines over it.

By late afternoon they were not there. John had to look hard and intently even to see where the gun was, although he had watched the whole process of putting it there.

During all this activity, the natives had wandered up from the thatched houses and stood around watching and then wandered back. They were brown-skinned, almost naked people who just stood and watched. The children, too, watched but soon lost interest and went back to their lagoon and their little dugout canoes.

When the gun was in place and the enemy settled in, John at last turned and went back around the point.

The presence of that long-barreled and wicked gun was all he could think about as he sat under his tree opening the coconuts that had fallen and drinking the thin but good juice.

In all of his and Jeff's elaborate planning—for the radio and food and medicine and gasoline and spare parts and a stove—*all* of it, they had not included this gun. They had simply skipped over this time (which was now measured in only hours) between his landing on the island and the flight to drop the gear. Skipped it.

So that now he could not tell Jeff about the gun. If he lit one fire on the beach that night it would tell Jeff that he was okay. If he lit two fires it would tell him to send a sub or PT boat to take him off—that he was not okay.

There was no way, however, to tell him that he, *Jeff*, was the one in danger. That the enemy had come that day and set up the gun and were now, in their dirty green uniforms, waiting for him to fly within range of the gun. Which, with the wind blowing from the east now, Jeff would inevitably do.

As night fell on him, he wandered out on the lonely beach and looked south toward Guadalcanal and the *Enterprise*. Right now, he thought, Jeff's engine is turning up. In a moment the flight deck officer will be whirling those flags for the full power turnup. In another moment he will slash the flags for take-off, and Jeff will be rolling down the deck of the Big E, his SBD loaded down and heavy with all the gear he was bringing to his brother.

For a long time as he sat on the beach, the little waves lapping over his bare feet, he could not think beyond the gun.

But as he felt the time of Jeff's flight melting away, he forced himself to think and to decide.

He must assume that the gun would fail. In that case what should he tell Jeff with the little fires (and they must be *little* for the enemy was close at hand now)?

It must be one fire only.

If he lit two fires to signal that he could not stay there, Jeff would whirl the plane without dropping anything and hurry back to get help to get him off the island.

It must be one fire so that if the gun failed, Jeff would drop the radio. With that he could then tell Jeff about the gun.

John got up in the darkness and went back under the palms. He gathered an armful of the dried fronds and carried them out on the beach. Since there was no hurry he stacked them carefully as he had learned as a Scout. That done, he went to the Mae West and got the waterproof container of matches.

Now there was nothing to do but wait until ten o'clock.

The moon came up at 9:45, and John lit his fire and waited until it was burning well and then with binoculars and pistol he went back under the palms and walked again around to the other side of his island. There he sat down against the same tree and looked across the channel at Choiseul. In the native village the little lights were burning, the flickering of them reflected in the water below the houses.

But of the enemy there was nothing. To a man in a plane only the lights of the village would show; the lights and the gray-brown thatch of an innocent village which could do you no harm.

At first the sound of the SBD was far, far away but it

came on steadily, growing louder and louder. To John it sounded as loud as thunder, as loud as war. No one could sleep through such a hammering from the sky. All of them over there would be up and running to the gun.

They were. Through the binoculars he could see the dark shapes of the enemy scuttling from the jungle and disappearing into the pit with the gun. But the gun did not yet appear.

Jeff did. The SBD swung slowly in from The Slot, flew close to the mountainous top of Choiseul and then, lined up, came floating down the valley, losing altitude all the way.

Now the gun appeared, its long, dark barrel emerging from the black earth and pointing skyward, moving this way and that, slowly and viciously.

The SBD appeared now in the sky. John slammed the binoculars on it and as he did, he saw the big diving flaps coming down, moonlight shining through the grapefruit-sized holes in them.

It was so *low!*

And just *floating*. Jeff was leaning it out, leaning it out until you wondered how the plane could stay in the air at that slow, floating speed.

The gun waited.

The plane floated down until it seemed to John to be less than a hundred feet above the black surface of the jungle. And there it hung, floating along, the engine droning in the silent sky.

The gun opened with a shocking, startling loudness. John could see the muzzle blast but that was all. The bursts of the antiaircraft shells were concealed by the darkness of the mountains behind them.

The plane floated on, coming straight in over the gun emplacement.

It passed over the gun and kept coming straight toward John and the island.

As it kept coming, not faltering, not flaming, not altering its course or swaying in the sky, John heard himself yelling with pure joy and relief.

"Drop it and get out of here," he yelled up to his brother. "Get out, get out!"

The SBD flew directly over him so low and close that he could hear not only the engine but the hiss of wind around the dive flaps.

"*Gun* it, Jeff!" he yelled, turning in the sand to watch the plane as it flew over the jungle behind him.

Suddenly, with no warning, no nothing, the shape of the SBD, dark-gray and graceful in the sky, changed. With an explosion which almost knocked John down, the SBD changed from an airplane into a ball of brilliant yellow, white and black fire which continued to float through the sky, leaving behind it a rolling column of black smoke which twisted its way up toward the calm moon in the vacant sky.

John could only stand there, tears now running down his cheeks, and watch his brother go. The light of the flames lit the beach and the jungle, fading only slowly away as the plane, now falling, cleared the island and crashed into the waiting sea.

And then there was no longer the sound of flames and minor explosions, nor the coughing dying of the engine.

There was only the faint, faint sound of men cheering.

John turned slowly around and slowly raised the binoculars. Over there in the moonlight beside that gun, little men

were hopping up and down in celebration, their cheers floating across the silent channel.

John said, "I'm going to get every one of you."

Then he knelt down in the sand and cried.

4

It was a long, cruel night for John Lawrence. The shock of
seeing his brother die like that was so great that he did
not remember going back around his island. He remembered
seeing the fire he had lit dying, leaving only a glow on the
beach, but he did nothing about it, going on to his Mae
West and his tree.

There he sat down, sick and weak and crying in his heart,
but there was no peace. The mosquitoes came, and numbly,
he put on his socks and flight helmet and goggles and then
plastered his face with the mud.

And still there was no peace for it began to rain, the
drops cold and soaking. The rain washed the mud off his
face so that the mosquitoes could feed on him again, and
he remembered thinking, "What do the Marines on Guadalcanal do when it rains?" So he did what they did, lie flat
down in the mud, his face down in it, leaving only enough
mud cleared away so that he could breathe. The cold rain
poured down on him from the trees above.

Gradually, as the shock wore off, he began to realize bit
by bit where he was.

In that last day on the *Enterprise*, John Lawrence had
erased himself not only as an officer in the Navy but as a
person. Carefully, step by step, he had arranged it so that
no one aboard the ship would miss him, or wonder where

he was or come looking for him. He had done a good job that last day.

Only Jeff knew.

And Jeff was dead.

Nor now could his voice be heard. All those careful plans for the radio; setting it up for the Marine's frequency, getting the right crystals from Hicks, packing it so that water could not reach it, nor shock break it, nor the sea swallow it—gone, all gone in that one great, horrid, floating ball of fire. Gone with Jeff. So that now any cry for help from John Lawrence would only be heard by the birds on his island, and the crabs and mosquitoes and all the rest of the crawling, creeping and flying things.

No food.

Only the soaking clothes he had on now.

Only the ending of the rain and the rising of the sun kept the awfulness of his situation from overwhelming him.

The long night ended and the long day began.

Hunger now actually hurt him as he got himself up out of the mud and scraped the slimy stuff off his clothes with his hands. It made him nauseous and weak, and the water he drank out of the cleanest puddles he could find did nothing to help.

In the Mae West was a packet of fish hooks, some line and some yellow and red silk to make a lure.

John was turning to the beach and the sea with these, hoping to catch a fish or find some sort of shellfish, when the sound of the enemy's motorboat drove him back into the now hot, stinking and dripping jungle. Hidden there, with bugs crawling on him, he looked out at the sea and saw the boat bucketing along, parallel to his beach.

In the bow were two men, manning a mounted, thin-barreled machine gun. More men, in steel helmets, were crouched in the boat, lining both sides of it.

For one dead man, John thought, they do this?

The boat began to circle in the area where Jeff's plane had gone down—around and around senselessly—so that John, driven by hunger, forgot them and went on through the jungle.

As he fought his way through the tangle of vines and bushes, he tried to remember when he had eaten last. Yesterday? The day before?

He could not remember when, only where. In the wardroom of the *Enterprise*, surrounded by other officers. There was white linen on the table, and silver service with USN stamped on it and stewards serving the food. He hadn't eaten much, he remembered; he had been too excited about erasing himself from the Navy and going to that island so that he could again get into the war.

The going through the jungle became easier then, and in a little while, he seemed to be following a winding, overgrown path leading up to the summit of the island.

He was walking along this when a vine or something caught him around the ankle and threw him flat to the ground, ramming the holstered pistol painfully in against his chest. At the same time, throughout the jungle there was a sudden, short, tinny, rattling sound.

But when he got up he found that it was not a vine which had tripped him, it was a length of rusty wire.

Backing away from it, John got the pistol out and ready, his eyes searching the jungle for any enemy.

There was only the wire and as he followed it with his eyes, he saw that it had been carefully placed there and was strung out through the jungle, supported by small stakes driven into the ground. Hanging from the wire at intervals were rusty, empty tin cans. The nearest one he found held a few pebbles.

This trip wire had been put there for a purpose, but as he waited, he heard no alien sound and saw nothing moving in the jungle ahead.

He was too numbed by hunger and defeat to care much whether he was ambushed or not. He went carefully enough, the pistol ready, and keeping to the side of the path, but nothing happened.

Except that he had a sudden premonition and it saved his life.

He stopped walking suddenly and with one foot began to explore the ground ahead, sliding his foot out over the matted leaves and branches and new, green, tender ferns.

The ground dropped out from under his foot leaving a deep, yawning pit.

He moved cautiously to the edge of it and peered down. The pit was ten feet deep and ten wide and lay straight across the path. Standing upright in the bottom, coming up like men at attention through a foot or so of water, were long, viciously sharpened and burned stakes. A man falling in there would die after awhile, impaled on the stakes.

Now he began to be really careful and cautious. Creeping around the edge of the pit he left the path, but keeping it in sight through the tangle of jungle, followed it on up toward the top of the island.

The house was so cleverly camouflaged that he walked into the wall of it and tried to make his way through it before he recognized what it was.

The house was made entirely of thatch from the jungle and blended in completely with it. John had torn a hole in it and now, through it, he looked into the house itself.

It was just a shack with some sort of grass matting covering the floor. There was an Army cot with a ragged mattress still on it, a table and a chair, some rusty tools in one corner, and hanging from the walls, some clothing. It looked completely deserted and long unused, but he was careful to be quiet as he walked along the wall and to the door, which was made of thatch also. He pushed this slowly open with his foot and then stepped back waiting for a shot or a rush.

Nothing happened and John at last walked into the little house.

A man lay on the floor, face down. He was dressed in a ragged khaki shirt, khaki shorts, ankle-high boots. The bones of his arms and legs and neck and head lay bare and dry.

John backed away in horror and then came forward again and looked more closely, for this man had been dead a long time. Even the great stain on the grass matting was dry and fading.

Then John lost interest in the man entirely, for stacked along one wall of the house were tin cans, some still having tatters of paper labels on them. John circled the skeleton and picked up one of the cans. Taking it out into the filtered sunlight of the jungle, he tried to read the label but could not.

Getting the dagger he had liberated from the Marine Guard on the *Enterprise*, he tore into the can.

It held some sort of dryish, condensed meat which tasted to him like the finest food he had ever eaten. Slumping down against a tree, John worked the can all the way open and then ate the stuff without even wondering what it was or whether it was good to eat—or even designed to be eaten. It tasted good and he ate it.

Feeling much better he went back into the house. Taking

a rubber ground sheet from under the mattress, he put it down beside the man and then with a rusty shovel got him onto the sheet, rolled it up and carried him out into the jungle where he left him and went back to the house.

In a crude shelf made of driftwood there were a few dog-eared and half-destroyed books. There were also a small gasoline stove, a few dishes and pans and metal utensils, a lamp and some candles, a ruined flashlight, the batteries melted out of it.

On the table was a canvas bound notebook with, beside it, a stub of a pencil. John opened the book and found that it was a diary, short entries for each date. He flipped through it to the last entry, which was in June. The writing, in contrast to the rest of the book, was feeble and sprawling and said:

"Old 3B 'as 'ad it. And I've 'ad it. I don't think I'll last the night the way it's going. If anyone finds this, please get in touch with my wife in Cherter Street, Melbourne, and tell her I'm dead so she won't be wondering the rest of her days. Tell her that Michael got away with Tingalap, but I have not heard from either since. And tell her that all my life I tried to accomplish something, to be somebody and never made it. But if Michael lives I'll go out happy because all my life I loved her."

John put the book slowly down and looked out the door at the bundle in the rubber ground cloth.

The man had neglected to say what his name was, so how could anyone ever tell his wife that he had loved her.

John thought to himself that he and that man out there could have been friends, for they would have understood each other very well. To accomplish something, to be somebody . . . and fail. Always fail.

He pulled the chair up to the table and started at the front of the book.

Only a few entries were clear. The rest of them were written in a sort of abbreviated code which meant nothing to him. Jottings like:

"Had a do with dink on freq X."

"Pet low and getting lower."

One entry dated three weeks ago was clear enough.

"Talked with Dink today. The Japs are closing in everywhere so it is time for Michael to go. Tingalap will take him as far as Tulagi—God'll have to do the rest. How strange it feels to a man to send his son away like this into a world he never made. But if he stays with me he will surely die, as I will. So he must chance it."

John sat in the little house and wondered if the dead man's son had escaped.

Another entry was clear, too.

"Heard that the Nips mopped up the U. S. Navy around Midway. So what's to stop them from taking the States and then with Germany and the Eyeties, taking Australia? Is the whole world going under? I'm glad I won't see that."

The next entry read:

"Pet all gone, boohoo, and forgot to tell dinkum. Yamasaki snooping about again. Would adore to shoot the barstid but would wreck whole setup."

What did it all mean? What was that man doing here? Who—or what—was "dink" and "freq X" and "3B" and "Yamasaki" and "pet"?

John leafed through the book again, trying to find a clue. The man must have been an Australian . . . so dink might mean dinkum. Did that mean "good"? "Okay?" Or a nickname? And "Pet getting low." Pet . . . Petrol . . . Gasoline? But what would he need with gasoline? For the stove? The lamp?

And then like baseballs thrown by a fast pitcher, two words hurled themselves out of the book:

TALKED and *HEARD*.

5

Two hours later John had not found the answer. He had searched the little house and the jungle around it. There he had found many empty and rusted tins with the words "5 Imperial Gallons" on them; he also found a dozen cans of 30-weight engine oil.

There was—or had been—then a motor here somewhere. But where it was now he could not discover. Nor could he figure out many of the entries in the diary. "3B" and "freq X" remained meaningless, although he wondered if "freq" could stand for frequency?

As he searched he kept seeing the ground sheet lying where he had left it and at last he stopped searching and went to work to bury the unknown man. With the rusty shovel from the house he started digging a grave under one of the big trees nearby.

He had dug down about a foot when the shovel struck metal and with a hollow sound.

John dug hard then and in a little while, he had uncovered five metal chests. In one there was a radio receiver. In another a series of six-volt wet cell batteries. In a third a loud-speaker. In the fourth there was a transmitter. Scraping the oxidation off the name plate he solved the mystery of 3B. The plate read:

Teleradio Model 3B, Manufactured by

Amalgamated Wireless, Ltd.

Melbourne, Australia.

In the fifth box there was an air-cooled motor to drive a small DC generator.

John stood in the jungle and looked at salvation lying there useless at his feet.

No gas. "Pet low . . . pet gone." No gas, no motor. No motor, no charge for the batteries. No charge, no current in the tubes, no radio. No voice crying from this island that John Lawrence was here.

He buried the bones of the man in the grave made deep where the chests had been and then he lugged the radio and batteries and motor into the house. Inside one of the chests he found a complete manual on how to operate the motor generator as well as the radio.

The antenna and ground for the radio had been so beautifully hidden by the man that John would not have found them if he had not known that they must be here somewhere. The lead-in from the antenna had been worked in under the bark of the tallest tree, and when John traced it up the tree, he found that footholds had been cut into the trunk so that it was easy to climb. At the top there was a little wooden platform from which John could see all around the compass.

From this height he could look down and easily see the enemy's camouflage over the gun, and see their tents and the native village.

He could also see far out across The Slot.

Then he whirled around and looked again at the enemy. There under the trees, concealed by the splotched greenish tarpaulins, were the crates and boxes and—barrels. There would be gasoline over there. And the only thing in the world that could save his life was gasoline.

PART FOUR

THE GUN

1

John moved into the little house in the jungle, but when he got through you could not tell it. He wanted it that way—for the house to look deserted and unused—so that if Yamasaki (whoever he or she was) should come "snooping about" again, there would be no trace of John Lawrence. He buried the Mae West and hid his little supply of gear where it could not be seen.

Through with that, he took his gun and the binoculars and climbed back to the platform in the tree to see if he could solve the problem of gasoline.

First he looked at the channel lying between his island and Choiseul. He studied it first for current and measured the movement of a piece of driftwood as it floated down the channel. The current was not a threat to him. Nor was the width. It would be a good, long swim for anyone but not impossible.

What had that falling-apart aviator said about bathing in the waters of Guadalcanal? "If the crocodiles didn't get you first."

John studied the channel and the shoreline for a long time but saw no sign of crocodiles. He noticed, too, that the native children swam and played in the water without apparently any fear.

He decided at last that the channel, although an obstacle, could be crossed in relative safety. There was, of course, the always present threat of sharks, but with these he would simply have to take his chances. What else there was to threaten him in that water he did not know.

Next came the gasoline itself. Once on that beach with the unseen enemy all around him, he would have to move fast and know exactly where he was going and what he was doing.

Through the glasses he could see the piles of their supplies covered with the greenish tarpaulins, vines and leaves. The piles were scattered around haphazardly in the jungle, and it was impossible for him to tell where they had put their supply of gas.

For over an hour John sat on his little platform and studied the enemy. He watched them going about their chores—gathering firewood, filling more sandbags, working around their tents. One group seemed to be uncrating supplies and restacking them, but he could not tell exactly what they were working with. Another group came and went around the gun, apparently bedding it in permanently. Two men worked in the motorboat, tuning the engine and swabbing it down.

Finally the gun itself appeared as they ran through what he guessed was a General Quarters drill.

John sat and minutely studied that gun. As he moved the glasses over every inch of it, he tried to remember what he had learned about Jap artillery in the Ground School at Pensacola. As it gradually came back to him, he decided that this was one of their three-inch guns. Unlike the AA guns on the *Enterprise*, this one was hand-loaded with a sliding breechblock which contained the firing pin and trigger mechanism held in place by the breech lock.

After GQ all the enemy assembled on the beach. Stripping off the dull-green uniforms, they went into the water and frolicked around.

John sat in the top of the tree and watched and counted them. There were not as many as he had first thought: twenty-three.

Sitting there he suddenly remembered what Winston Churchill had told the people of Great Britain when it seemed that the Nazis were going to invade England. "Take one with you," Churchill had said.

"I'll take more than one," John whispered. "If I can I'll take them all."

As long as they were playing around on the beach there would be no solution to the problem of where their gasoline was stored, so he turned the glasses on the native village.

The houses were curious affairs. Apparently the natives were too lazy to clear a space in the jungle to build a house—or perhaps, he thought, being more generous, there was some threat in the jungle that they wanted to avoid. At any rate, the houses were built around long stakes driven into the bottom of the sea. They were all out over the water and about ten feet above it. From the center of each house a crude, steep stairway (really more a ladder) led down to a platform just above high water.

Tied up to the platforms were the natives' boats. Long, graceful, low dugout canoes made from one log. They were of various sizes and the ones that John particularly liked were the children's—these little boats were marvelously made and even more graceful than the big ones. And the kids were masters at moving them. The kids in the boats buzzed around like mellow bugs, their broad-bladed paddles flashing in the sunlight. The kids were all naked as jaybirds and when they weren't darting around in their boats, they were in the water swimming like fish. To John they looked totally happy and totally unconcerned by the enemy so close beside them and the great war being waged all around them. Just swim and paddle those boats and yell with joy— he could hear their shrill voices faintly as he could also hear the hoarser voices of the enemy.

As far as he could see, the native women did all the hard work. True, a few men were gathered in a clearing in the jungle and were hacking out a log for a canoe, but at the rate they were going, John estimated it would take another hundred years to finish it. On the other hand, the women labored hard and endlessly in other clearings, digging and planting and carrying. They went back and forth like ants carrying huge bundles of wood for fire and other things they dug up or gathered which John could not identify.

He was watching all this when from the corner of the glasses, he saw a movement in the jungle above the village. Swinging over to it, he saw a young boy coming down a path with a tall man behind him.

John watched them coming, and as they came into a clearing he saw that the boy was white. He looked to be about fourteen or fifteen with a shaggy mop of uncut, sun-bleached hair and just tatters for clothes.

John was then startled to see that the tall man behind the boy was carrying a rifle, pointing it at the boy's back.

Michael.

Somehow John knew that this boy must be Michael, the dead man's son who had been sent out into "a world he never made."

It was a good thing, John thought, that his father is not here to see this, for the tall man now struck the boy with the rifle, forcing him to turn toward the enemy encampment.

The soldiers gathered around the two and John saw the tall man stoop and cut away the ropes at the boy's wrists.

Then there was some sort of confusion which John could not make out—the men suddenly started milling around and yelling.

And suddenly running for his life, the boy burst out of the group of men, running toward the water.

John had not until now hated the enemy as individuals, as persons. At Midway he had been afraid of him; he didn't *like* him and he despised him for his treacherous attack on Pearl Harbor. Even the killing of his brother had not been a personal thing; it had been done with a gun in a war which had been declared. But now he felt a deep and personal and real hatred for this enemy.

He sat in the tree and watched as the boy, almost naked in his tattered clothes, ran splashing into the water. And John watched the tall man with the rifle raise the rifle and shoot the boy in the back. John saw the muzzle flash and the boy stagger and fall before he heard the sound of the shot.

The boy lay face down in the shallow water as the men started running across the beach toward him.

And then the boy began to move. To swim. John almost stood up on the platform and cheered.

The soldiers ran back to their rifles and soon turned and began to shoot at the swimming boy, their bullets making white splashes all around him.

John sat there whispering, sending out to the boy all he

could. "Get under the water! Get *under!* Go . . . Go!" But the boy did not and in a moment he stopped swimming. His arms did not appear again, and there was only his sun-bleached mop floating away.

The firing from shore tapered off and stopped. Two of the men started running toward the motorboat, but another of them beckoned with authority, and they stopped running and came back to stand with the rest watching the boy's head floating out toward the middle of the channel—and floating on toward the Coral Sea.

Now there began a curious, high-pitched wailing coming from the village. John swung the glasses over there and saw that the men had all gathered on the shore and were more or less milling around in a group, some carrying spears and decorated shields. But they made no move toward the enemy. From the houses came the high-pitched keening of the women, and for once the children were still and quiet.

John swung the glasses back to the channel.

The boy had disappeared.

For a long time he sat there studying one by one the faces of his enemy—men who could shoot a defenseless kid in the back.

"I'll take you with me," he said again.

As he watched and hated them, they went back to their duties, the tall man returning to the village. Two of the soldiers caught John's attention as they walked away from the rest.

John held the glasses on them, hoping, for they were the same two who had started to man the motorboat.

The two soldiers, laughing together as they walked, went toward the stores piled in the jungle. Passing most of the camouflaged dumps, they came to the end. One of them began carefully lifting away the vines and leaves and the other pulled an edge of the tarpaulin up.

This was the first time John had been able to see this particular pile of stores and he liked what he saw. Shiny tin was bright in the sunlight, and as the man got the tarpaulin clear, the other one lifted down from the top a rectangular can—exactly like the rusty ones marked 5 Imperial Gallons.

John was beginning to shake with excitement as he watched the two men take down four of the cans and set them to one side.

He cursed them for lazy slobs as they slowly and carefully, and with much laughing and horsing around, pulled the tarpaulin back into place and taking forever, put the vines and leaves back over the pile.

At last—and John found he had been holding his breath— they each picked up two of the tins and started walking away with them.

They dawdled. They played around. They put the tins down and sat on them, resting, so that John in the tree could not yet tell what was in the tins—he could only hope that his very life was in them.

The two vicious clowns at last reached the motorboat. John let out his held breath again. It *must* be gas. It *had* to be gas.

It was. They opened the tins, and while one held a funnel, the other carefully emptied the tins in the tanks of the motorboat.

There would be no point, John argued to himself, in putting twenty gallons of water aboard the boat. And what else besides gas would come in such tins and be put into the tanks of a motorboat.

So there it was.

John climbed stiffly down out of the tree and went into the little house.

For a while he just sat in the chair staring at the radio.

Across the channel was gasoline. He would have to swim across it, steal the gas and swim back.

Simple.

It would have to be done at night, of course. And he did not yet know what sort of patrol the enemy kept at night. Nor could he be sure that there were no crocodiles in the channel. There were a hundred things which could stop him from getting that gas.

But he was going to try.

John spent the rest of the daylight working on the little motor. With the operator's manual on the table he went over it step by step (admiring as he did it the completeness of the manual and remembering the skimpy manuals for U.S. machines—ninety per cent of the manual being advertising.)

When he finished he could see no reason why the motor wouldn't run . . . as soon as he put gas in it. The plug was in good shape and he had gapped it according to the manual. It had spark—he found that out the hard way by holding the spark plug wire with one hand and yanking the pull cord with the other. Lots of spark. It had oil and turned over nicely with good compression. The batteries also looked in good condition although almost dry. The next time it rained he would rig up some way to catch it in the empty tins and get the water level up in the batteries. But, he thought, once he had gas the batteries would operate long enough to get at least an emergency SOS out to the Marines.

So as the sun set, John went back to his tree and the long study of the enemy.

2

This night was dark and threatening, and he remembered the five day forecast of the meteorologist on the *Enterprise* as the heavy clouds of storm began to gather and tower above the mountains of Choiseul. (Good man, that meteorologist. Recommend him for a Navy Cross.)

The moon came up but he saw it only for a little while as the sky now clouded completely over and left the world below almost pitch-dark.

This helped him in one way and hurt him in another. Although he had not yet seen any sign of an enemy patrol, he could not now in the pitch darkness see anything at all. He would not know whether or not they posted a patrol late at night.

That, he argued, was just another of the many perils he had to face.

And one minor problem which worried him out of all proportion to its importance. What to wear for this occasion? Full uniform? So that if he was captured he would be complying with Navy regulation number so-and-so. But to swim the channel and back in shirt and trousers would just add unnecessarily to the already difficult passage. His flight suit? Although it wasn't as heavy, wet, as his uniform would be, it would still be a tremendous drag on him during a swim of that length. One thing he knew—the white skivvies were *out*. The enemy could see those things shining like a visiting ghost.

The Mae West was out, too. It was a fine device to keep you from drowning, but to push it through the water all the way across the channel and back would take him all night and all his strength—and possibly more.

There was nothing for it but to comply with Navy regulations by wearing his dog tags. After two days spent almost entirely under the blazing sun, his already tanned body was now almost black in the darkness.

Dog tags, shoulder holster and gun with ammo, a belt so that he could take the sheath knife. He'd wear his shoes down to the beach, but the rest of the way would have to be barefooted.

It began to rain as he climbed down the tree and this changed his plans a little. He had decided to wear his flight suit to the beach so that the mosquitoes wouldn't eat him alive on the way, but the flight suit was at last dry, so why get it wet again? If the mosquitoes wanted him, they could have him, John decided, running for his pitch-black little house.

In the darkness there he stripped off everything but his shoes and socks. His dog tags were very non-regulation, for his mother had been much offended by the crude aluminum discs the Navy issued him and had had made beautiful, thick silver tags, wonderfully engraved and hung on a heavy silver chain. John had not had the heart to point out to his mother that the Navy tags with their stiff string were much lighter and more comfortable, and if you were caught in a plane on fire, the string would burn away whereas the silver chain would only heat up and brand you. So he had worn his mother's gift, hoping that his plane would not catch on fire.

He put on the heavy chain and then the holster, then the belt and knife and went out into the rain.

Skirting the staked pit which he had re-covered during the day, he went slogging down the path to the beach. There he went out on the sand for it was easier walking in the rain and darkness, and the rain would soon wash away his footprints.

On the other side of the island he could see only a few feet out into the rain. The enemy camp, the village, even Choiseul with its high mountains, were invisible through the rain.

Taking his shoes off, he went back into the fringe of palms and picking out a curiously twisted tree, buried his shoes at the foot of it, hoping as he did it that he could find them again sometime.

Now he was ready as he walked slowly back toward the sea, the cold rain pouring down on him.

John hesitated for a moment to fight back a wave of fear which suddenly began to roll over him. Everything was so black and menacing and except for the falling rain, so silent. Even the sea had been subdued by the rain so that there were no waves with their cheerful restlessness.

He had to remind himself that without gasoline he could not long exist. And without it he had no real purpose being where he was. Or, he thought, being alive at all.

Suddenly, in the rain he began to laugh and at the same time wade out toward the deep water of the channel.

In the last letter he'd gotten from his mother, she had been much amused by the latest antic of the Government. Now, she had written, everyone had been issued a sticker which you were supposed to put on your car's windshield— put, she had said, where you could always see it, whether it interfered or not with seeing what was *outside* the windshield. The sticker asked you in big red letters: IS THIS TRIP NECESSARY?

The sea was much warmer than the rain. He waded out waist-deep and then stopped and stood there feeling the wind blowing against him. He slowly turned his head from side to side, lining himself up with the beach behind him. Then he turned his head slowly once again until he felt his face cutting the flow of the soft wind. He would, he decided, keep the wind just there so that he would know which way he was going, for in this rain and darkness it would be easy to get lost and wind up swimming forever through the Coral Sea or land on Choiseul somewhere far away from the enemy.

Then he began to swim. He swam steadily but not fast, for he had a long, long way to go and wanted to get there. The warm water flowed past his naked body, and when he looked back after a little while, his island had been swallowed up in the rain and night.

So he swam, stopping regularly to find the wind with his face and if necessary, change direction to keep it where he wanted it. He did not let himself wonder what else was swimming in the water with him, deciding that that would only frighten and tire him and he could not afford that.

The holster and gun began to chafe him but he went on, since there was nothing he could do about that.

There was nothing he could do about time or distance either. With the pouring rain he seemed to be swimming always in the same place, with the same sound—an almost dry rattling as the raindrops struck the sea.

John was beginning to worry, almost to panic, for it seemed to him that he had been swimming for far longer than it should take to get him across the channel when his stroking hand touched bottom.

He stopped then and let his feet down. With just his head above water he tried to see through the rain but could not. "They can't see me, either," he said to himself and waded slowly forward.

Then in the rain he saw the motorboat's hull under the

camouflage and felt a sudden rush of elation. He had come perfectly across the channel—right on course.

He drew the pistol, slipped the cylinder open and made sure water drained out of the barrel, then closed the cylinder. The last thing he wanted to do was shoot the thing, but if a patrol jumped him in the darkness he would, he decided, have to shoot.

He waded slowly and quietly out of the water and crouching down on his haunches, peered through the rain for landmarks and also watched and listened for any sign of a patrol.

There was none. After a little wandering he found the stack of gasoline tins.

Now he was very careful to make no noise and to lift the tarpaulin so that he could put it back exactly as it had been.

With the tarpaulin lifted off, the tins seemed very bright even in the darkness.

Being careful not to let them strike together, he lifted down two tins from the top tier and set them on the ground. Then he moved the rest of the tins in that row, moving each about an inch so that when he finished, he had filled the gap left by the two he had taken.

Yanking the tarpaulin down again, he picked up his ten precious (and he assumed Imperial) gallons of gas and went back to the sea.

As he waded out he panicked for a second, wondering whether gasoline was heavier or lighter than water. If it were heavier his two tins would drown him.

He remembered then (with some embarrassment) that gas was much lighter than water. The tins would hold him up, not drown him.

He hurried a little now and was soon swimming.

To hold his direction was more difficult now for he had to feel the wind on the back of his head, which was not as sensitive to the light wind as his nose was, but he was so happy to have the gas and not at all tired that he thought he could afford to swim far off course if eventually he got back to his island.

He was wrong. The only way he could make any progress was to lie on his back, holding the tins of gas by the handles, one with each hand, so that he could use only his feet for swimming.

It was endless, and he was at the point of total exhaustion when the back of his head struck a sandy beach.

John could barely hold the tins from drifting away as he lay in the shallow water and gasped for breath. At last he got enough strength to drag himself and the tins out of the water and safely up the beach. There he lay down in the rain and was sick.

He thought of hiding the gas in the jungle and coming back for it tomorrow, but in the rain and darkness he was afraid that he could not mark the hiding place so that he could find it again.

It took all his will power to pick up the tins and stagger southward along his island. The thin metal handles were cutting cruelly into his hands (he cursed himself for forgetting to wear his flight gloves) and he had to put them down every few feet and sit on them and pant before he could go on.

The walk along the beach was bad enough, but the climb up the pitch-dark path was pure torture. Not even the knowledge that he had gasoline at last and that each painful step was bringing it closer to the radio transmitter and rescue helped to make that struggle up the path any easier.

In the dark his foot struck against the trip wire, rattling the tin cans eerily through the jungle and also throwing him face down and hard into the mud.

He got up after awhile and remembering the pit, skirted it and walked on toward the little house which he could finally see.

He could not carry the tins any further. He let them drop into the mud and staggered in the door of his house. He shoved it open with his shoulder and stumbled into the dark silence.

John was on the verge of collapsing on the floor; his knees were giving way, his body slumping down, when the pain struck him.

It started in his right cheek and flowed down it to the curve of his jaw. It stopped for a split second and then began down his right shoulder and breast, stopping finally at the wide, thick leather of the shoulder holster.

He was so exhausted that he could not for a moment think clearly at all. Just a great, searing pain had run down him—pain he could not even seem to wonder about.

But when it began again, striking him now along his left arm, he staggered away from it, slamming against the doorjamb and spinning on out into the dark rain.

And then at last he could think—a little—again.

Someone was inside the little house. Someone with a knife.

3

Almost falling, he backed away in the rain and now could taste the sweetish taste of blood being washed into his open and gasping mouth by the rain.

He backed into a tree and slid down it and sat, his back against it, his legs sprawled out in the mud.

The pistol was wet and slimy with blood, but when he got it out of the holster the rain made it only wet.

John sat there stunned and exhausted, staring at the dark opening where the door was. He could feel blood pouring out of his wounds but he had to wait here helpless in the rain, until something came out of that door.

Slowly, as he forced himself to think, he decided that whoever was in there was armed only with a knife. Otherwise they would have shot him when he came in.

A gun against a knife.

That made him feel better.

Not getting up, he twisted over onto his hands and knees and crawled away to the left until he was out of sight of the door. Then he turned back and crawling silently through the rain and mud, got to the wall of the house. He crawled along it to the door and then stopped again.

Cautiously, he leaned forward far enough so that he could see into the house. It was pitch-dark.

Then he remembered that he had hidden the silly little red flashlight that came with the Mae West in the thatch just inside the door.

With the flashlight, silly or not, and the gun, he would be in a far better position to defend himself.

He reached in slowly and found the flashlight and brought it out. His fingers were now so stiff from carrying the tins of gas that he had to take both hands to get the flashlight into his left hand, his thumb on the switch. Then, getting the gun in his right hand, he leaned forward again, keeping his body away from the door, and poked the flashlight into the house with his left hand, the gun with his right. Then he swung his head in and turned on the flashlight.

The thin little beam of light fell directly on a dark figure crouching in the far corner of the room.

And as John started to pull the trigger, he saw in time that it was the tow-headed boy crouched there. He was staring at him, and John could see now that he was far more frightened than he was.

But the kid had a knife—a crudely made thing but with a long and sharp blade.

He held the light steadily on him as he slid his body up to the door and then slowly got to his feet, the gun steady on him.

Then the boy's eyes closed slowly, and he fell slowly back against the wall and kept on falling until he was lying in a heap on the floor, his fingers falling open from around the knife.

"Michael," he said. "That's your name, isn't it?"

He started over to him but then remembered that this kid had been running from the enemy for weeks. Remembered his courage there on the beach. This boy was brave—and dangerous.

Still holding the gun on him, John scraped the knife out of his hands with his bare foot. The boy didn't move.

John put the flashlight on the table so that its beam fell on the boy and then picked him up and put him down on the cot. Blood oozed from a bullet wound just below his rib cage, and when John gently turned him over, there was another oozing wound in his back.

Australia puts out some pretty rugged kids, John thought, remembering his own swim across that channel. This one had done it with a bullet wound all the way through him. Added to that, he had gotten back to his father's house and for good measure had had strength enough left to almost kill him with that knife.

But, John wondered, was the kid rugged enough to live much longer?

Going back into the rain he brought in a tin of gasoline. As he carefully opened it with the Marine knife, he thought how foolish and defeated he would feel if it turned out to be molasses—the same way he had felt years ago in Pensacola when the plane nosed up with him and left him hanging by the seat belt.

It was gasoline. He filled the Coleman lantern with it and pumped it up. The mantle was still intact, and in a moment the lamp was hissing away quietly, the mantle throwing out a startlingly bright, white light.

There was so much light that, in fear, John ran out into the rain and walked all the way around the little house. With the thatch door closed no direct light came out of it—only a dim, diffused faint glow coming through thin places in the thatch. He doubted if the light could be seen for ten feet through the jungle.

He went back in and looked at his own wounds in the Mae West signaling mirror. At first the blood streaming down his face and chest scared him sick, but when he wiped it away he found that a good deal of it was rain and that the kid hadn't seriously damaged him. The long cut down his face and chest had only sliced open his skin, the one down his left arm was hardly more than a scratch.

He got the rubber ground sheet and went back to the boy. Lifting him up, he slid the sheet under him and then put him gently down again.

The bullet had gone cleanly through him, leaving no more opening where it came out of his belly than where it went into his back. John was a little surprised by this as he had heard that the enemy was not using full patch bullets but were illegally shooting people with lead slugs that would mushroom in you and blast a crater coming out.

John didn't like the slow oozing of blood from the two wounds. He took the Marine knife over to the Coleman and let the point of it get red hot in the flame. When it cooled, he went back to the boy and cut the wounds open so that his blood began to flow out of them.

When the flow began to stop, the blood congealing, he got the first-aid kit in the Mae West and took out the little packet of sulfa powder, sprinkling it on the wounds. Tearing up his shirt, he made pads to put against them and taped them on.

During all this the boy never moved or showed any sign of pain, but he continued to breathe.

That was all John could do. Using the rest of his shirt soaked in rain, he swabbed the blood off himself and turned back to the gasoline.

He was so exhausted now that he could not keep from shaking. When he tried to pour the gas into the tank of the little motor, he spilled some of it.

Tomorrow, he decided. Everything tomorrow.

It seemed to take all his strength to pull the flight suit up over his wet body and then to close the long zippers. He looked at the boy once more before he turned the lamp out, lay down on the floor and within seconds was sound asleep.

4

Some sound or movement woke him up. The rain had stopped and sunshine was streaming in through the open door. John lay on his back, his bones and muscles aching, and looked at the sunshine.

Then another sound caught his attention and he turned his head.

The tow-headed boy was crawling toward him on hands and knees. John had never seen such a blaze of hatred in anyone's eyes as the kid weakly raised the Marine knife and tried to stab him.

He rolled out of the way of it and sat up.

The kid kept coming, the pain of it so great that his face was the color of a dirty sheet.

"Michael," John said.

For a moment it didn't register through all the pain and horror, but when it did the boy sat weakly back on his haunches and looked at John with sick, begging eyes.

"Your name's Michael, isn't it?" John asked.

The boy just nodded. And then he began to cry. He put the Marine knife down on the floor in an oddly deliberate, careful way and put both hands over his face so that John wouldn't see that he was crying.

John got up. "You're okay, buddy," he said, lifting the limp boy up and putting him back on the bed. The boy turned his face to the wall and went on crying.

John knew how he felt and left him alone. He filled the little tank of the one burner stove with gas and almost blew his hand off lighting it. But when he got the flame down to a reasonable size, he got one of the battered saucepans and then opened one of the tin cans. It was soup of some sort. He put that on to heat and turned back to the boy.

He had stopped crying and was lying on the cot looking at him.

"You're a Yank," the boy said.

John was surprised but then remembered the leather name tag sewed to his flight suit.

"Where's my father?" the boy asked. "This is my father's house."

John pretended to be busy with the soup. Nobody had ever told him how to do a thing like this. To kill a little boy with a couple of words. But suppose he lied to him now, wouldn't that just make it harder to take later on?

John turned back around and went over to stand beside the cot. "Your father's dead, Michael," he told him.

The boy didn't cry. He closed his eyes for a moment and then slowly opened them.

He didn't cry but his face turned that dirty-sheet gray again. He tried to be a man but his voice came out very young and small. "He had to, didn't he?"

"He had to," John said.

Then John saw that blazing light starting to glow in the boy's eyes. "Did they kill him?"

"No, he was sick."

"He had malaria," the boy said, matter-of-factly. And then the blaze died away and his eyes began to shine and his voice grew stronger. "My father had malaria so bad that anybody else wouldn't have been able to move. They wouldn't have been able to even lift up their *little* finger. But my father got up out of this bed every night and climbed up the tree and stayed there no matter if it rained or anything. And if he saw something he would climb down and radio it in. Nobody else could have done that."

"He was a good man," John said.

"Umm," the boy said. "He was a good man." Then the boy turned his face toward the wall. "I'm going to die, too," he said.

John had never felt so helpless, so *useless*. "Hurt pretty bad?"

"Not any more," the boy said. Then he began to cry again. "I'm sick, Mr. Lawrence. I'm sick all over."

John's throat was so tight he couldn't talk. *Mr.* Lawrence.

"You want some soup, Michael?" he asked in a little while.

The boy didn't answer. John leaned over him and found that he had either passed out or gone to sleep. He was breathing, but it was very shallow and fast. John laid the back of his knuckles against the kid's forehead and was startled by the dry heat of his skin.

But there was nothing he could do. Nothing.

John sat watching the boy as he ate the hot soup. Finished, he went outside and buried the can.

When he came back in the boy had not moved. John picked up the opened tin of gasoline, and now he was steady enough to pour it into the gas tank of the motor without spilling it.

He stoppered the tin with another piece of his dwindling shirt, screwed the cap back on the gas tank, turned the petcock on as the manual instructed, choked the carburetor three-quarters, held the motor down with one hand and reached for the pull cord.

As he started to pull he was already talking to the Marines on Guadalcanal.

He pulled the cord hard and straight back. The flywheel spun, the piston worked, the crankshaft turned, spark flew across the gap of the plug—and nothing else happened.

He pulled it again and again. He pulled on that cord until his right arm grew tired and numb, so he pulled on it with his left until that, too, grew tired and numb. He went back to the manual, reset the volume and needle valves, rechecked the motor and pulled some more. It would not start.

He worked on it all morning and then, exhausted, panicky, soaked with sweat, he stopped long enough to eat the soup in the other can (wondering, in a towering rage, why so much *soup?* Why not some more of that meat he had found in the first can?).

The boy was beginning to writhe on the bed and to moan pitifully in his sleep, but there was nothing he could do to help him and he needed this motor to run as much as John did.

Desperation made his efforts to start the motor uncoordinated and defeating. He tinkered with this and that. Pulled the cord. Tinkered. Glared at the offending thing and cursed it and even slapped the motor with his open hand.

5

That boy was dying, John thought, as night fell over his little island and the obstinate brute of a motor. He lit the Coleman and stood with it in his hands, looking down at the boy. Although he was conscious, he was in such agony that he was incoherent, just a writhing mass of agony on the bloody bed.

John suddenly remembered the morphine Syrettes in the first-aid kit. As he got the little glass vial out, he tried to remember what the doctor had said when he was telling the aviation cadets how to use the kit. But his flight training days in the battering sun of Pensacola seemed centuries away and vague as forgotten dreams.

He broke the glass at the inscribed mark and filled the cylinder about half-full. Taking it to the boy, he held him still with one knee and then, holding his arm with one hand, jabbed the needle into the inside of his elbow and watched the clear fluid flow into him.

In a few minutes the morphine took effect and he lay in a sort of stupor, his eyes open and watching John but, John could tell, not intelligently.

His total failure to start the motor had at last driven him to slow and patient desperation. With the Coleman on the table and the tools neatly belted into the box the motor had been in, John took the thing apart, creating an oily but orderly mess on the table.

There was absolutely nothing wrong with that motor.

This pushed him to the bottom of defeat and he just sat there staring at the rows of parts lined up on the table.

A memory drifted in and drifted out. One Sunday afternoon in Pensacola, he and another aviation cadet had rented a boat with an outboard motor and had gone tearing around in the Bay. And then the motor had stopped, and like this one, he could not get it started.

After an hour or so of cord-pulling and tinkering, they were in trouble, for both of them had so many demerits that to be late for another muster or, worse, to miss a bed check would get them thrown out of the Navy.

The old guy with the beat-up boat and battered motor who finally came along had been about as untalkative as you can get, but he had said one interesting thing as he climbed into their boat and looked at their motor.

"Hit's got gas," the old man had said, "and hit's got f'ar so hit's bound to run."

And it had run, and they had made the muster with seconds to spare.

He had gas and he had fire so, *this* motor was bound to run.

Piece by piece he put it back together again as the boy finally went to sleep, but not quietly.

And then in the middle of the night, John found a piece of flaked-off paint about the size of a dime which had fallen past the butterfly valve of the carburetor and had lodged across the venturi throat.

John sat there staring at the flake of paint on the end of his oily finger and wondered about life and death and a good many other things.

A little piece of old paint had been lying between his life and his death. And perhaps that boy's life, too.

He hurried now but was careful and thorough, and when it was all together again, it ran like a clock.

It packed the little house full of muffled noise and exhaust fumes and bad smells, and John loved it and gave it a pat and said nice things to it as he connected the generator end of it to the batteries and then impatiently waited.

He took the case off the 3B and turned the Coleman down. Stopping the motor he switched the radio on.

The filaments glowed faintly, and in a moment the speaker began to hum.

John turned the tuning dial of the receiver, and so suddenly that it startled him, a woman's voice, very pleasant and low, said, ". . . and today sank the United States Navy's aircraft carriers *Enterprise*, *Wasp* and *Saratoga*. The intrepid pilots of the Emperor of Japan also sank . . ."

John tuned her out, recognizing her as Tokyo Rose, an American girl turned traitor for the Japanese. He had heard all that before. Heard her say that his ship, the *Enterprise*, had been sunk at the Battle of Midway. How, he wondered, could those intrepid pilots of the Emperor sink the same ship twice? Clever, they were.

He knew, as he fiddled with the tuning dial and listened to broken sentences and spurts of Morse, that he was simply putting off the time when he must test the transmitter. Putting off the time when he would find out finally whether his voice, crying for help from this dark island, would be heard.

And there was no use putting it off any longer. He turned to the transmitter, pushed the lever from REC. to TRANS. and leaned toward the microphone built into the front of the set.

What, now that the time had come, was he going to say? He realized with sudden embarrassment that he had not even thought about it until right now.

He leaned forward again. "Calling Guadalcanal," he said slowly. "Calling the U. S. Marines on Guadalcanal. This is radio X, calling Guadalcanal. If you hear me please come in, Guadalcanal."

He flipped the lever up to REC. and slowly tuned it. There was no answer.

He suddenly felt like a fool. They could be answering right now on a thousand different kilocycles. He set the receiver on 900 kc. and went back to TRANS. "Guadalcanal, this is radio X. If you hear me, please answer on 900 kilocycles."

Marvelously, incredibly, like a voice from Heaven, a man from Brooklyn, New York, said, "This is radio Guadalcanal. Who are you, radio X?"

John was so overwhelmed by this sound of a voice that he blurted out, "I'm John Lawrence, a jaygee in the Navy. I'm up here just off the tip of Choiseul. I. . . ."

Then he stopped talking suddenly and felt sick from his own stupidity. He realized too late he had just committed suicide. If the Marines on Guadalcanal could hear him, so could the enemy at Rabaul or even right across the channel on Choiseul.

I'm a fool, a stupid fool! he cried to himself.

And the voice came from the loud-speaker. "Radio X, this is Guadalcanal. Who are you?"

John stared at the lever. It was positioned on REC.

He saw that his hand was shaking as he reached out to the little, smooth and shining lever and pushed it over to TRANS.

"Guadalcanal, this is radio X. Do you read me? Over."

He switched back to REC.

"Radio X, this is Guadalcanal. I read you five by five. Who are you and where are you?"

"Never mind who and where," John said. "I will have information for you about junk in The Slot and June Bugs over it. You dig me? Over."

"Radio X, hold everything. Stand by. Over."

John sat staring at the humming loud-speaker until in a little while another voice came from it. This one was not from Brooklyn and it was full of authority. "Radio X, this is Guadalcanal. Who are you?" It wasn't a question, it was a demand.

"Guadalcanal, this is radio X. It does not matter who I am," John said again slowly. "I will have information for you."

There was a dry, derisive sound from the speaker and the voice of authority said, "I get all sorts of information from you bastards all the time. Who're you kidding? Out."

John heard the Guadalcanal radio click off.

It infuriated him. Those stupid Gyrenes!

He slammed the lever to TRANS. "Guadalcanal! Get with

it, you slew-footed, idiotic Gyrenes. You may not want to live forever, but how about tonight? Radio X, over."

The dry, derisive laugh sounded again, oddly personal and close from the metal cloth covering the loud-speaker. "You slant-eyed, yellow-bellied little man," the voice said. "You're keeping me up."

John slammed the lever back. "Now, listen, you stuffed-shirt Marine. Go ask Bill Hunter in Navy Operations what happened to him one night in the San Carlos Hotel in Pensacola, Florida."

The voice was not quite so derisive when it answered. "So you spikka da langwidge. So do a lot of the rest of you. What have you got on your mind?"

And then John heard it. The faint, vibrating, unsynchronized drone of many planes.

"Guadal! Stand by! *I mean this!* Stand by. Over."

He ran out into the dark and climbed the tree as fast as he could, the binoculars swinging back and forth against him.

And there they were, twenty-four Vals in three Vs of eight. They were low and dark and fast as they swept past the island going south. He could see the streamlined pants over their unretracted wheels and he could see, too, the bombs slung below the fuselages.

He hurried down from the tree and into the house.

"Guadalcanal. Radio X. Do you read me? Over."

"Five by five," came the voice.

Then John started to blurt out that twenty-four enemy bombers of the Val type loaded with bombs had just passed him heading south at fifty-feet altitude, ground speed 140 estimated. But for long seconds, he said nothing.

John had suddenly realized that to be effective here he

must survive. The enemy must not know what he was saying for then they would also know where he was.

"Now, read me, Dad," he said slowly, mentally changing 140 knots' ground speed into minutes to Guadalcanal. "Vals at angels fifty with a century so move the frenzied felines, crud or no crud."

"Say again," the voice said.

"Over and out," John said, listening to the Vals going away as he flipped the radio off and went outside.

And in the radio shack on Guadalcanal, a Marine corporal from Brooklyn stared at a hollow-eyed Marine major who was intently picking scabs out from between his fingers. "Guy lost his mind, I guess," the corporal said.

"No," said the major. "At least, I hope not." He went to a field phone and cranked it hard. "Operations? Hunter? Field, here. We just got a weird radio message. A guy said something about a night you had in the San Carlos Hotel. And then he said, 'Vals at angels fifty with a century so move the frenzied felines, crud or no crud.' Mean anything to you?"

Hunter, in operations, had another attack of the dry heaves which had been bothering him lately so couldn't answer the major. When he could talk again he tried to crank the phone but was too weak, so a yeoman third staggered over and managed to twist the handle hard enough.

Hunter said, "Just got a report that some Vals will be here in ninety minutes—make it eighty-five. So scramble as many Wildcats as you can get pilots for. Plan to be on top by zero two fifty. May be an enemy gag but let's ride it."

He hung up the phone and collapsed on a filthy cot to whose legs had been strapped some pieces of lumber to keep the cot from sinking completely into the mud.

The San Carlos Hotel: He tried to remember but could

not. It was all so long ago and far away—another world. Which he was sure he would never see again so why bother about it now?

And so he never thought again about the San Carlos Hotel and the night he got, shall we say, a little tiddly there, and only good ol' John Lawrence saved him from the shore patrol and being thrown totally out of the Navy. Saved him for Guadalcanal in the Solomon Islands in the Coral Sea where in a few days, Bill Hunter would die.

In the radio shack the corporal said to the major, "I wonder who that guy is, making with the slurring remarks about the glorious United States Marine Corps of which I wish I'd never heard nothing of."

"Corporal . . . pardon me, I mean, Private . . . I think radio X is as phony as Tokyo Rose. So the next time he starts making with the remarks, you put the RDF on him and find out where he is and I'll send a man to get him. A man with a little gun."

"Major," the corporal said. "Pardon me, I mean, Colonel, sir. I hope you're not serious with the "private" routine. I got some children and a very sickly wife."

The major laughed as much as men laughed on Guadalcanal and said, "Just remember to nail him with the RDF, Sergeant. And since you were married yesterday, how did you come by all this family all of a sudden?"

And at zero two fifty three, 24 Val bombers at 20,000 feet swung in from over Iron Bottom Bay and headed for Guadalcanal.

They got there—in pieces. The Wildcats, orbiting at 30,000 feet and piloted by men who were sick and wounded and tired, came down on them through the clouds and clawed them out of the miserable sky.

6

The boy didn't die that night, but when John looked at him in the morning he didn't think he would last another night. John did what he could to help him as he lay there looking up at him. The kid's eyes were so full of hope, full of confidence that he would save him, that John had to turn away.

He decided that he would bury the boy beside his father. Perhaps someday, he thought, I'll find a woman in Australia who is waiting for her husband and son to come away from these stinking islands.

It started to rain around eight in the morning and he welcomed it. Going outside, he got the rusty gas tins and set them under the eaves of the thatched roof so that the rain dripped down into them. As soon as he had enough, he carried it into the house and carefully filled the batteries. Then he patted the motor affectionately, spoke to it with praise, pulled the choke, set the throttle and yanked the cord. The motor started and as soon as it smoothed out, he set the throttle for maximum charge and left it running.

He opened the last of the cans—it was soup—and carried some of it over to Michael, but he only shook his head and turned his face away from it. John sat down in the chair and watched him as he drank the soup out of the can and wondered where his next meal was coming from.

With the almost daily rains, water was no problem but now food was.

It was so simple and so frustrating. Right now he could flip the transmitter on and call Radio Guadalcanal, and they could fly a crate of food up to him by afternoon. Only that gun stood in his way. He didn't want to see another airplane explode into a mass of fire and go into the sea as Jeff's plane had.

Before he could ask for help he had to knock out that gun, and now the twenty-three men over on Choiseul seemed far more menacing than they had when he had gone for the gas.

But it might be days, even weeks, before he could find a way to stop the gun and, in the meantime, he had to live on something.

The boy's voice startled him. It was weak and dry and hoarse. "Mr. Lawrence, can I have something to eat?"

John went over to him. The boy's eyes were closed now, and except for his breathing, he looked dead.

"All the food's gone, Michael," John said. "Is there anything to eat on the island."

The boy didn't open his eyes but his voice was clear and strong. "Daddy," he said, "can't I play for just a little while longer? Just a *little* while?"

"Yeah," John said. "Go ahead and play, Mike. I'll call you when supper's ready."

The boy smiled a little but did not open his eyes.

John wandered out of the little house and stood looking at the mass of the green jungle. Somewhere among all these vines and roots and leaves there was something to eat. The natives over there on Choiseul didn't have cans full of soup. *They* lived off this jungle.

Words came to him—"taro" and "sago," "pandanus," "cassava"—but the words had no meaning, no identification with the stuff growing around him.

Then he thought of the sea and went rushing back into the house for the little fishing tackle kit that came with the Mae West. He got it out, tied one of the hooks to the nylon line and put the rest of the gear in his pocket.

The boy had started that writhing and moaning again, the pain drawing his face into lines as he ground his teeth against it. John decided that this was as good a time as any to give him the rest of the morphine.

As he slipped the needle into Michael's arm, he couldn't tell whether he was conscious or not. He didn't seem to feel the needle at any rate. And as John checked the motor and battery charge dial, the boy became quiet and still.

John thought: If he ever comes to again, I'll ask him what his last name is. He would need to know that in case he ever got off this island.

He decided it was safe to let the motor go on charging the batteries until it ran out of gas. The exhaust was so muffled that even with the pipe sticking outside the house, it made very little noise.

Down on the beach in the rain he scoured the sand for bait but only found it back under the palms where after a good deal of running around, he managed to catch one of the big land crabs. And decided, as he took it apart, that if he couldn't catch a fish, he would investigate these critters and see if they were good to eat. The crab's meat looked a little unsavory, but John was getting hungrier by the minute.

He waded out into the water, baited his hook and flung it out as far as he could. Then he waited.

He waited and waited and the fish, if there were any, ignored him. Nowhere along the beach, or even beyond it where the thick green bushes grew out into the water, were there any hungry fish.

He gave up finally and went back after the crabs, which he could see wandering around under the palms.

He couldn't catch another one—and wondered how he had caught the first one. On those spindly legs they could go like lightning, and make a turn ninety on nothing at all. They could also be in clear view one second and vanish in the next.

After a good deal of crab-chasing, John had to sit down and rest. Hunger was now painful and he felt weak and dizzy from lack of food.

Giving up at last, he went back to where he had left the remains of the first crab only to find that the others had made off with it while he was fishing.

But there were coconuts lying on the ground. He gathered up as many of the best-looking ones he could find and slogged through the rain back toward the little house.

He remembered to step over the trip wire and noticed as he came closer, that the motor had stopped. Out of gas, he decided, wading on through the mud.

He pushed the thatch door open with his foot and the first thing he saw as he went in, his arms full of coconuts and water streaming down his face, was the boy.

He had pushed himself into a half-sitting position, his back against the thatched wall, and was staring at something with that blaze of hatred John had seen before.

Then the tall man stepped forward.

It was the same man who had led Michael out of the jungle. The man who had taken him among the enemy and cut the rope from his wrists. The same man who had shot the boy in the back as he ran through the shallow water.

He was dressed as Michael's father had been—in dirty khaki shorts, ankle-high boots with ragged socks, a short-sleeved, belted bush jacket also ragged and dirty, and a wide-brimmed Aussie hat.

Under the hat was a face John would never forget. It was neither Melanesian nor Japanese but a mixture of the worst features of both. A truly disgusting face of a muddy, yellowish color.

When John saw the gun in the man's hand he was numbed

again by that feeling of failure. It was his own gun, the Smith & Wesson .38.

"Lie down," the man said, "on your face." He pronounced it "fyce" like an Australian.

John hesitated for a second, debating. If he rushed him and got the gun, good. But if he got killed doing it?

There was no doubt in John's mind that the man would not hesitate to kill him. And at this moment, he was perfectly protected and alert. Too, since he had not killed him yet, perhaps he did not want to—now. So that later John might have a better chance.

He dropped the coconuts and then dropped to his knees.

"All the way," the man said. "On your face."

John stretched out on the floor, turning his face to the right. He could see Michael's eyes, still blazing, but in a moment the man's legs blotted out that view.

"Put your hands up on your back," the man said.

John obeyed him, hoping that the man would come close enough to touch. But he did not. He stood clear of John and leaned over, the gun in one hand pointing at John's back. He was doing something with the other hand which John could not see, but in a little while he felt something touch his wrists and as the man moved away, he felt a thin rope or wire tighten painfully around his hands.

The man became less careful then as he looped the rope around his wrists two or three times and then stooped at John's feet and tied his ankles together.

"Now you can walk," the man said. "But if you run it will tear your hands off if I don't shoot you first."

John was suddenly sorry that he had not gone ahead and rushed the man and taken his chances, for he knew now what was going to happen. The man would take him across to the enemy on Choiseul (the man, himself, may be one of them, he thought, but the clothes and the fact that he had come here unarmed were against that).

With them you died, but it took a long time during all of which you wished that you could die.

Finishing his knots, the man moved first to the radio and stood looking down at it. He touched the motor with his hand and John was delighted to see him draw it back in pain, burned by the still hot block.

The man turned then to the boy and stood looking down at him.

"Get up, Michael," he said, "and walk."

The boy shook his head weakly.

"Get up!" the man said, and reached down, grabbing him by one arm and yanking him up from the bed.

Then the man did a curious thing as he pulled Michael's body up against his.

First he turned him loose, and John watched Michael in agony as he fell back on the bed.

Then the man turned slowly around as though undecided what to do and walked toward John.

And then, slowly, he sank down on his knees and bent forward. He put the gun down on the floor with a careful, slow movement and with both hands, clasped his stomach.

Between the man's laced and now gripping fingers, John saw the dull-knurled hilt of the Marine Corps dagger with the little smooth ball on the end. Only a little of the hilt came beyond the man's fingers.

He died there without a sound and fell forward across John's legs.

John rolled away from under him and still rolling, got to the gun. He rolled on top of it and then lay for a moment looking over at the man.

He didn't need the gun. He twisted his legs around and

under and sat up on the floor so that he could look at the boy. He was still half-sitting on the bed, his eyes now closed.

John could see that he was going out fast.

"Michael!" he yelled at him. "Stay awake."

He could move faster just by pushing his feet against the floor. At the bed he got up on his knees, his back to the boy, and shoved his hands toward him until he felt his skin against his knuckles.

"Untie me!" he said. "Hurry up!"

Twisting his head around he watched and prayed, for Michael's eyes were closed and he was swaying from side to side.

But he felt hands on his wrists and after an agony of time and weak fumbling, he felt the rope's tension ease. Then Michael's head fell against his back and he slid on down him to the bed.

John worked his hands out of the loosened rope and then untied it from around his ankles. Reaching out he got the gun and then turned to look at the boy. Only his body kept him from falling off the bed, so he twisted around and gently lifted him back into the middle of it. He knew that he couldn't hear him now but he said, "Thanks," out loud.

He stepped over the dead man and went to stand against the wall beside the door. Outside he could hear nothing but the steadily falling rain and when at last he looked out, he saw no one.

John slipped out into the rain and moved over into some bushes where he crouched and waited, watching the path for as far down it as he could see in the rain.

He waited and watched for a long time but no one came.

The man must have come here by himself, John decided, and went back into the little house.

The man lying dead on the floor could now become even

more dangerous than he had been standing there with the gun. On Choiseul someone was waiting for this man to come back. And when he didn't come back they would come looking for him.

John knelt down and took off one of the man's shoes. Although the leather was not dry inside, it was not soaked through, either.

John sat on his heels, the shoe in his hands. The man had come by boat. Where was it?

He sat for a moment longer, thinking, and then he turned the man over, got the Marine knife out of him and began stripping off his clothes, his socks and his shoes.

Outside in the rain he held the belted jacket under water falling from the eave and scrubbed as much of the blood stain out of it as he could. There was nothing he could do about the hole the knife had made going through it, but he hoped that no one would notice the exact and neat little slit the thin, double-edged blade had made.

It was hard digging in the mud and ooze but at last he got a grave down deep enough. He dragged the man out by the feet, rolled him into it and shoveled the muddy earth back on top of him.

That done, he climbed into the top of the tree with the glasses and began to scan the beach of his island on the Choiseul side. It took him a long time to recognize the dugout for it had been well hidden among the tangled bushes (were these mangroves? he wondered), but at last he made out its darker shape among the dark-green leaves.

He was thankful for the rain and the low wisps of cloud slowly drifting above the channel, for he was sure that no one on Choiseul could see the boat hidden on his island.

Unless the man had told someone where he was going?

As John climbed down out of the tree, he felt the trap of

time closing around him. He wanted desperately to go right now and get rid of that boat, but he knew that he must wait until late in the night when they would be asleep on Choiseul.

But what if the rain stopped and the moon came out? Trapped!

To force time to pass John puttered. He refilled the motor's gas tank and started it again, letting it run as he then got some water and sluiced away the blood on the floor. He washed the Marine dagger as though getting it ready for an operation. He changed the bandage on the boy, using the last of his shirt. Then he tackled the obstinate coconuts, finally breaking them open all over the place with a rusty hammer.

As he sat at the table eating the moist, rather stringy and tasteless meat, he thought of the Australian's diary and thumbed through it until he found the entry about someone named Yamasaki. John was convinced that the man Michael had killed was Yamasaki and not one of the troops across the channel. Was he married? (John couldn't imagine any woman marrying a man with a face as repugnant as that, but then. . . .) Would anyone in those high thatched houses over there be sitting around the little lamps wondering where Yamasaki was? Or, worse, was someone right now going from house to house—or even to the enemy—arranging for a search party?

He tried to stop thinking about it and turned his attention to the battery charge dial. He watched the needle until it hit the stop and then cut the motor.

It was still raining, the noise seeming to grow louder as the sound of the motor died out of the house.

He had nothing to report to Guadalcanal, nothing really to say, but he turned the radio on anyway and sat waiting for it to warm up. He felt surrounded now by loneliness and death as he looked over at the boy who was quiet for a change, just lying there asleep.

He flipped the lever to TRANS. and said, "Guadalcanal radio, this is radio X. Do you hear me?"

In the radio shack on Guadalcanal, the Brooklyn corporal grabbed the microphone and as he talked to John, stretched the cord across the tent to where the major was asleep on the bed. He shook the major awake and handed him the mike.

"Er . . . um. . . ." The major cleaned his teeth with his tongue and blinked a few times. "Radio Canal here. Radio X? I read you five by five."

The corporal came close and said, "Keep him talking, major," and left the tent, running out into the rain.

"Peace on earth, goodwill toward men," John said. "To-night."

"You know it, brother," the major said. He looked toward the rain-soaked tent flap, but the corporal did not appear. "How's every little thing?" he asked in the mike.

"Can you keep a monitor on my frequency?" John asked.

"Anything to oblige," the major said, frowning as he wondered what was taking the corporal so long. "By the way," the major went on to John, "we rolled a good game last night. Left nothing but a baby split."

Then the corporal, dripping, came back in and nodded with a sly grin to the major.

"Must have good alleys down there," John said. "I'll send you another load of pins when they get here."

"Good boy," the major said to John and then whispered to the corporal, "Get it?"

"Got it," the corporal whispered back.

"Just checking my rig," John said. "So over and out."

"Good night, ol' buddy. Over and out."

The major hung up the microphone and hurried over to a table where the corporal was already laying parallel rulers on a chart of the Solomon Islands. He drew a thin pencil line from an X on Guadalcanal northward. It sliced through a tiny island with the secret code name Clementine and down the length of Choiseul and then out across the sea.

The major picked up a pencil and put the point down on Clementine. "He's either on this one or in the mountains of Choiseul. If he's here . . ." he tapped Clementine with the pencil, "he's a dead pigeon. If he's in the mountains I doubt if we can find him."

"Major," the corporal said tentatively, "what do we want to find him *for*?"

The major looked around surprised. "For? Suppose he's a Jap feeding us bad dope. Don't we want to know it?"

"Man tells us the Vals are coming so we've got time to get up there and knock down twenty of them. This is bad dope, Major?"

"What's a few planes if we begin to trust this guy on radio X? One night he'll tell us the whole fleet is coming down The Slot so we rush everything we've got up there to stop 'em, and they come in through Sealark and blast us off this island. Aren't a few planes worth that?"

The major didn't look it, the corporal thought, but he was a sharp Marine.

7

John sat for a moment longer looking at the still humming loud-speaker. He wished that he could go on talking to that dry, still derisive voice of the Marine on Guadal—just the sound of the remote voice made him feel less helpless, less threatened. But he was afraid to go on too long. If the enemy had any radio direction finders in this area, a long broadcast would pinpoint him and bring them down his throat.

He was reaching for the on/off switch when another and completely different voice came from the speaker. "Radio X, this is radio Y. Do you read?"

"Five by five, Y," John said. The voice had a heavy Australian accent and no derision.

"Is your rig an Amalgamated 3B, X?" the voice asked. "That's right."

Was this some sort of enemy trick? he suddenly wondered. He'd better be careful.

"Is the serial number 10789?" the voice asked.

John licked his finger and then rubbed it on the name plate. Through the oxidation he could read the number: 10789.

"Could be," John said warily.

"Don't get your back up," the voice said. "What became of Vance Carruthers?"

"Where'd he live?" John asked.

"In Cherter Street, Melbourne."

Just to make sure, John checked the diary. This was pretty convincing. "Who are you?" he asked.

There was laughter on the other end. "Careful, old bean. Must keep 'em guessing, you know."

John knew exactly. "Carruthers is dead. At least, I think its Carruthers." He started to say that Michael was alive but didn't. Why raise his mother's hopes?

"Poor chap," the voice said. "Last time I talked with him he said he was fading. Any news of his son Michael?" John looked over at the sleeping boy. "No news of him but Carruthers left a note for his wife," John said. "It says. . . ."

He started to read it and then changed his mind. "It says he died loving her. Can you get that to her?"

"Can do. Well, good night, old bean. You're doing a gooddo job . . . for a blinkin' Yank." There was a click and then nothing but humming from the speaker.

John turned the set off and sat there; the trap, which had been opened a little by the voices from the world he had left, closing down tight on him again.

From across the little room the boy said, "Mr. Lawrence?"

John swung around. He was half-awake and lying on his unhurt side.

John went over to him. "You feeling better?"

"I think so. Who was that talking?"

John wondered if he had heard, but the boy's face was so blank, so sick, he thought not. "Just the radio."

"Where's Yamasaki?"

"Outside. Dead."

"My father wanted to kill him," the boy said. "But my mother wouldn't let him."

"Is your name Carruthers, Michael?"

The boy nodded. "I don't think I'm going to die. I feel hungry."

John picked up a piece of broken coconut and got the meat out of it. "That's all there is."

The boy gnawed at the stringy, damp meat. "It's good. Are you a pilot?"

John glanced down at the faded gold wings on the leather name tag. "I used to be."

"What are you now?"

"Nothing," John said.

"Are you spotting the planes and ships the way my father did?"

John nodded.

"Well, that's not nothing. That's something."

"Yeah, I guess you're right." He dug out some more of the coconut meat and put it on the bed beside the boy. Then he handed him the knife the boy had brought. "I've got to go across the channel, Michael," John told him. "I might be gone a long time."

The boy looked at the knife for a moment and then up at him. "Are you coming back?"

John thought about the enemy and the gun and now the natives. "I'll be back."

"They'll kill you if they see you."

"I know." John flapped his arms slowly. "I'm invisible. See?"

The boy smiled a little. "I'm the only one can see you."

"When we get back I'll cook up something to eat."

"I'll help you. My father said I was a good cook."

"It's a deal," John said. "I'm going to have to turn the light out."

The boy nodded. "It's better if they come in the dark," he said. "I can see them before they see me."

"That's right," John said. "How old are you, Mike?"

"I'll be fifteen pretty soon."

John strapped the shoulder holster on and shoved the Marine knife down into the belt of his flight suit.

He tried to remember what it was like to be fourteen years old—goofing around in school, goofing around after school, goofing around.

Fourteen years old. Sitting on a beat-up cot so weak he could hardly stay there, but ready with nothing but a native knife to take on not just one but *all* of them—in the dark.

He picked up Yamasaki's clothes, turned off the lamp, said, "Get well," and went out into the rain.

At the dugout he stripped off his flight suit and shoes and

hid them. Then he unrolled the bundle of clothes. In the bottom of the narrow boat he set the shoes down side by side and stuffed a sock into each one of them. The rest of the clothes he laid out neatly across one of the thwarts. Finished, he looked at his work and decided that it was absolutely evident that Yamasaki had taken off his clothes while in the boat and had gone fishing or diving for pearls—whatever they did around here. And a shark had nailed him. No doubt about it.

Getting into the stern of the dugout, he pushed it out into the channel and began to paddle with the short-handled, graceful, wide-bladed paddle.

After he got used to the extreme tenderness of the dugout, he found it to be a marvelously swift and easy boat to move. A deep breath on the wrong side would turn the thing over, but otherwise it was quite a machine.

He paddled quietly through the rain until he could see the faint glimmer of the natives' lamps, or whatever they were, and then he slipped out of the boat, going straight over the stern.

Pushing it now and swimming slowly, he nosed it in toward the tall stilts and when he could see a house clearly, he turned the boat and kept pushing until it struck the little landing platform.

It made a satisfactory hollow thump. John turned it loose then and slid back behind one of the stilts. In a moment he heard voices from the house above, and then a man with a burning brand leaned down from the square hole in the floor. When he saw the boat, he yelled back into the house and came hurrying backward down the ladder.

John took a deep breath, let out half of it and slid under the water. Pushing with his feet against the stilt, he sailed away in the darkness and then turned to his right and swam hard under the water for as long as he could. When the pain in his lungs grew too great, he turned on his back and let his face surface. While he was getting fresh air, he turned and checked his course.

He went underwater parallel to the shore and not far away from it until he was well clear of the native village. Then he swam on the surface, but quietly and slowly, watching the shore all the time. At the enemy camp he lay in the water watching for anything to move.

There was no sign of a sentry anywhere, and as he crept out on the sand, he was careful of trip wires or other alarms, but there were none. There was nothing now between him and the gun except a bare area of low rough grass.

Being a Naval officer, he had never been taught the Marine method of crawling on your belly using your knees and elbows and keeping your butt down, but he soon invented that method as he went through the grass to the gun.

When he got there he noticed that something had been added—a heavy 50-caliber machine gun all set and ready to go with the belt threaded through the breech. John thought, If I have time I'll look into this, too.

At the camouflage net covering the gun he stopped and listened, putting his head down close to the opening. In the rain he could hear nothing and in the darkness see nothing. If someone was down in the pit with the gun, that was just too bad.

John started to draw his pistol from the holster and then changed his mind. The knife wouldn't be as effective, but it wouldn't make so much noise.

They had built steps out of sandbags leading down into the pit. With the knife out in front and held low, John went step by step down into the pitch-blackness of the pit. Rain seeped through the camouflage net and he could hear it striking the bare metal of the gun, but that was all he could hear.

In the dark he bumped into the gun mount, the knife making a frightening clang against it. John stepped back from it until he felt the wet sandbags against his shoulders and waited, staring into the darkness and then up the steps.

He saw nothing, but the clang of the knife hadn't helped him so he hurried now, feeling for the gun with one hand and holding the knife with the other.

He slid his hand down to the breech and found the handle. Pulling it this way and that until it worked, he slid the breechblock open.

Now he needed both hands so he put the knife between his teeth and with thumbs and forefingers felt for the sharp finger slits he hoped would be there. And found them. Slipping his fingers into them, he twisted the mechanism to the right and felt it moving out into his hands. It felt like a big, cold, metal sausage.

He took the knife out of his mouth and then to be sure, ran a finger over the thing in his hand. He could feel the rounded point of the firing pin and then the spring of the cocking mechanism. They would undoubtedly have spare firing pins and even, probably, spare cocking springs, but not the whole lock case. That gun was now no more dangerous than any other hollow tube.

He almost felt like singing as he went back up the steps and crawled over to the machine gun. Squatting down in front of it, he slipped the stiff canvas boot off the muzzle and packed as much mud as he could down the barrel. Then he put the boot back on and moved to the other end of the gun. Pulling out one of the rounds of ammunition, he turned it around and slipped it back into the little canvas loop. That, he thought, ought to jam it for fair.

He was turning away from the gun when his knee struck a low, metal box. If he had not been so happy about his work with both the guns he would probably have gone on, leaving the metal box alone, but on this night he felt successful; he was accomplishing things.

He opened the thin tin top of the box and in the rainy darkness saw the hand grenades packed inside like the fancy fruit you got at Christmas time in the States. Neat little grenades all lying peacefully in excelsior which he was letting the rain in on.

John sat back on his haunches and looked at the grenades. Then he took one of them out and examined it. It was smaller than the U.S. grenades he had seen but seemed to work the same way—you put your finger in the little ring, pulled on it and the pin came out, and in a few seconds (he had forgotten now how many) off it went.

John sat in the mud with the rain falling on his head and looked beyond the gun pit. There, dark shapes in the darkness, were their tents. Six of them, roughly in a line. Four men to a tent, he figured, with only three in one of them.

Suppose, he thought, they do have a spare breech lock case? It would only take a minute or so to put that gun back into operation. And suppose the mud he had rammed into the machine gun barrel was simply pushed out by the first round fired instead of blowing out the back of the gun? Or— since the enemy was not stupid—one of them ran a bore-clear check on it and spotted the mud? And found the reversed round in the belt?

John asked himself silently: What have I accomplished here? Right now these two guns were useless, but in minutes they could be just as lethal as they had been when Jeff floated over in the SBD and the long gun got him.

It wasn't the guns, John now argued. It was the men. The

men now sleeping in those six tents while he sat in the mud in front of an open case of a couple of dozen hand grenades.

Suppose the Marines sent a plane up here with the food and other supplies he needed and those sleeping men had fixed their guns? It would be Jeff and the SBD all over again.

John sat in the rain and thought about it.

Twenty-three men. They would all have to go at once. So that ruined any ideas he had about throwing a grenade into each tent. By the time the first couple of grenades had gone off, they would be piling out of the rest of the tents. If any of them lived they'd get him, now or later.

So they all had to go.

But how?

He sat and looked at the now wet grenades and then closed the lid of the box.

How?

John's elation began to ebb, his feeling of accomplishment to drain away. Why, he cursed himself, hadn't he thought this thing out? "Completed staff work" the Navy called it. Why couldn't he ever do anything *right?*

The answer to how was so simple, but he had wrecked it by stuffing mud down the gun that could have wiped them out with one long burst. The only way to get that mud out now was to find a ramrod and ram it out. And where was a ramrod in all this mud and rain and darkness?

But he kept thinking of the grenades.

And then it came to him. Completed staff work.

He crawled over to the camouflage net over the gun and examined it with his fingers. Then with the Marine dagger he slashed some of the cords at both ends of it. After a good deal of fumbling and untangling, he at last went back to the grenades with two long lengths of cord.

Measuring with his eyes as well as he could in the dark, he tied six of the grenades to one of the cords, spacing them the distance he estimated it was between the tents. Then, cutting the other cord into six equal lengths, he strung these around his neck and started off with the six grenades on the string cradled in his arms.

If anybody takes a shot at me now, John thought, with this armful I'll go up in a blaze of glory.

But no one shot at him as he went beyond the tents and tied one end of the long cord to a tree.

Now he moved very carefully along behind the tents. At each one he put a grenade down as close to it as he dared— so close that at one tent he heard snoring and at another some man mumbling to himself in a dream.

He tied the other end of the long cord to another tree, drawing it tight and tying it well.

The hard shakes were bothering him now as he started back up the row of tents, and he had to stop for a moment and control himself before he could go on, tying the shorter lengths of string to each of the firing pin rings.

He almost collapsed with relief as he got the last string secured without any sign of the enemy.

There was no need for caution now—or too late for it. He stood up, the six short strings in his hand, and backed away until the strings came taut. Without pulling any more he shifted three strings to each hand.

And now that he was ready, the thought of killing these men while they slept struck him hard. It made him sick and ashamed of himself and he stood in the rain debating about it. Would it make any difference in the end if he now called to them, woke them up; even let them start to crawl out of those tents. Would that make their deaths any less complete and sudden?

And then John thought of his brother burning to death in the SBD and he pulled the six strings, feeling the six pins sliding out of the keepers.

He turned then and ran for the sea, his head turned back watching the dark tents, waiting for the blazing explosion.

It didn't come.

He felt the clean sand under his bare feet and then felt his ankles splashing into the water.

He stopped now and turned and looked back.

The dark rain fell on the dark tents and the man mumbled on in his dream and some snored, but there was no other sound except the rain falling on the taut canvas of the tents.

The grenades went off so close together that it was almost a single explosion—a great blazing, hammering blast and burst of brilliant light.

John instinctively dropped face down into the water and even at that distance, felt the air rush across his back.

Then it was gone. He lifted himself out of the water and looked back.

The rain fell into empty darkness. The tents had vanished and all was dark and soundless except for the falling rain.

John turned slowly away and went into the sea.

8

John was about to walk into his little house when he suddenly remembered the boy. And Yamasaki.

He stopped well clear of the door and called out softly, "Michael? It's me—John Lawrence."

There was no answer. Probably asleep, John thought. He reached cautiously in and got the little flashlight. Switching it on he beamed it at the cot.

The boy was not there.

And a voice from behind John said, "I could've killed you easy."

John swung around with the flashlight and the boy was standing there in the rain, the long knife in his hands. He was grinning up at John.

John slumped against the edge of the door. "Come in out of the rain," he said.

As the boy came in, he said, "I heard the explosion and I wasn't sure who was going to come over here. So. . . ." He waved the knife around. "What happened?" he asked then, wiping himself with an old shirt.

"I set off grenades beside their tents," John said, wiping rain off his face with his hands. Then he added, "They were all asleep."

There was a moment of silence in the house and then the boy said quietly, "I don't suppose it matters."

"I guess not," John said, lighting the Coleman. "I got the gun, too."

"Did you get anything to eat?"

"No, I didn't," John said, turning on the radio. "But never mind. Now the Marines can fly us up some food from Guadalcanal."

"Are the Yanks on Guadalcanal?" the boy asked, surprised.

"Sure. They've been there since early August."

"And the Japanese let them stay?" the boy asked, incredulous.

John turned around to look at him. "*Let* us?" he asked. "We *took* it from 'em, The U. S. Marines." But as he turned to the radio he added, "At least, we're in the process of it."

"You whipped them?" the boy asked. "That is very good news indeed."

"Now," John said, flipping the lever to TRANS., "I'll order

us a steak dinner with the whole works." He leaned to the microphone. "Radio Guadalcanal. This is radio X. Come in, Guadalcanal."

The corporal, barely awake himself, woke up the major. "Go ahead, Radio X," he said and looked at the clock hanging above the transmitter.

"Guadalcanal, this is X. I need food badly and medicine. Please ask the Marine airwing to air-drop supplies."

The corporal looked for instructions from the major but the major, throwing a poncho over his shoulders, went out into the rain.

John hoped that his singing voice had improved as he flipped over to TRANS. "Radio X to Guadal. Now watch the bouncing ball," he said. Then he began to sing the old song. "Oh, my darling, oh, my darling, oh, my darling, you-know-who. . . ." He sang as much of it as he could remember and then flipped to REC. There was no answer.

The corporal was out in the rain, yelling, "He's on Clementine, Major." But the rain was beating so hard on the major's poncho that he couldn't hear. The corporal went back in and wrote it all down as John told him what he needed in the way of food, medicine and supplies and asked for an air-drop the next night. When John signed off, the corporal called the colonel's tent and talked to the major, asking if he should tell operations.

The major sounded tired and belligerent, and sick. "No, corporal. We don't know how he got the name Clementine. And that's a real old gag. We send a plane up there and fly low and slow for an air-drop, and they blast him. Call Skimmer One on Tulagi and when you get them, transfer the call here."

"You going to send *them* after him?" the corporal asked.

"What are you bucking for—private?" the major said and hung up the phone.

Officers, the corporal thought. Where did they make them, Passaic? They looked like people but they weren't, really. He got on the short wave and called Skimmer One on Tulagi.

The major showed up again in a few minutes, and after one look at him, the corporal knew that it was time to keep his big mouth shut.

"That Navy," the major said in total disgust. He mocked a combination Harvard-Back Bay Boston accent, but not very well. " 'I'm vedy soddy, Major, but I'm afraid I cahn't do it. I have a mission coming up.' What's he running over there, the Salvation Army?"

The corporal kept his big mouth shut.

"I'm sick," the major said in a sad little voice.

The corporal looked over at him. Right now the major looked almost human as the hard malarial chills hit him and knocked him quaking and shivering back on the dirty cot. The corporal went over and put the stiff blankets on him and watched the major's trembling shake them off. So he put them back on and laid the wet poncho crosswise on top of them and let the major shake.

For a moment, knowing that the major, although he was wide awake, couldn't hear or wouldn't remember, the corporal was tempted to call up radio X and tell that guy that he was sorry but no food or razor or anything else was going to be air-dropped to him. But then, the corporal thought, why get my tail busted for unauthorized transmissions? It might be Guadalcanal but it was still the same old Marine Corps, and he'd been a buck private more than several times without ever being a sergeant.

John switched off the radio and turned happily to the boy, but he was fast asleep on the cot. John tucked in a fold of the mosquito net, turned out the lamp and climbed the tree.

That boy, he thought as he settled down on the platform, is going to get well. All he needed now was food and, John thought, by this time tomorrow night we'll have all the food we need.

9

The pitiful noises of his own hungry stomach woke him up, and he was surprised to find that it was broad daylight.

There were six shining round discs where the tents had been—rainwater, he guessed, in the shallow craters. The natives from the village were standing around, looking at them, or wandering around looking at the guns. Some of them seemed to be searching the beach and the edges of the jungle for tracks, and John was glad that it had rained as long as it had. There would be no tracks.

Over in the village two or three people were standing on the platform below one of the houses and looking at Yamasaki's dugout, while out in the channel there were three dugouts moseying around.

When he looked back at the enemy encampments, he saw that the natives were now attacking the supply dumps. They must have decided that the enemy had been whipped and were helping themselves, running back and forth from the piles to the village like crazy ants. In an hour, he knew, there would be nothing left. But it didn't matter, he thought happily, for tonight a plane would drop food for him and the boy—and medicine, and a razor.

As he was about to climb down from the tree, a movement on the other side of his island caught his attention.

It was Michael bathing in the sea.

And two nights ago, John thought, I gave that kid up for dead. Rugged, these Australian types.

He and the boy ate coconuts for breakfast and didn't mind, for there would be steak for dinner. After breakfast the boy went to sleep and John took off through the jungle alone, looking for the rubber boat he had dropped on this island that night now so long ago. He would need that boat if the air-drop missed and the stuff landed in the sea.

He couldn't find it, and by sunset he was a mass of swollen bites from insects, scratches from thorns, and weak and dizzy from hunger. As he stumbled back to the little house, he was met by the boy coming down the hill for more coconuts.

"We don't need 'em," John told him. "As soon as it's dark a plane will come with food."

And soon after dark there was the throb of a plane. As John ran for the tree he said, "I take back everything I ever said about the United States Marines. Well, *almost* everything."

In the tree he searched the southern sky, trying to pick the darkness of a plane out of the myriad stars but could find nothing.

He had expected the plane to come from the south, from Guadal, and so they were almost on top of him from the north before he saw them. Three more Vs of eight Vals each. They were so low they shook the tree as they went over him, making his platform sway. In the light from their exhaust stacks he could see the red meat ball on the fuselage.

He went fast down the tree and ran into the house, flipping on the radio without even noticing the boy.

He said, "They've come?"

John shook his head. "Later."

"Radio X calling Guadalcanal," he said into the microphone, keeping his thumb and forefinger on the TRANS./REC. switch. "Radio X calling Guadalcanal."

The Marine corporal was sitting on the other cot huddled in blankets and shaking so hard his teeth were rattling. As he pulled himself across the room and slumped down at the radio table, he looked at the major completely covered with blankets—just a shaking mass of O.D. cloth.

"This is Guadalcanal. Come in Radio X."

"Radio X," John said, "eighter from Decatur three straight passes."

"I read you," the corporal said.

"So buy me a steak dinner. Over and out."

The corporal sat for a moment letting a wave of the shakes sweep over him, and then he cranked the phone. The major and the colonel had about convinced him that radio X was operated by the enemy, and all that brass could be pretty convincing. On the other hand, the corporal thought, the high brass hadn't believed that radar operator early Sunday morning at Pearl Harbor and look what happened—3000 good guys got killed and ships sank like suds down a drain.

"That you, Murph?" he asked into the phone. "Well, tell Lieutenant Hollow-head I just got a message from radio X that twenty-four bombers were coming in, in an hour and a half. But don't tell him I said so. . . . *Who* said so? What's *your* authority? Listen, you bell-bottomed swabby, tell him you dreamed it. But just leave me out of it. We are having an unofficial chat at the expense of the Government. Over and out like a light."

He got the phone back into the leather case but couldn't make it back to the cot, slumping down across the table instead.

John and the boy sat in the house and waited then. They were too hungry and sick and tired to talk much, and sometime after midnight the boy said apologetically, "Mr. Lawrence, would it be all right if I went to sleep for a little while?"

"I'll wake you up when it comes, Michael," John told him. But he knew somehow that the food was not coming tonight. Tomorrow night for sure, he thought, fixing the mosquito net around the boy.

Tomorrow night for sure.

So that long night slowly passed and the next day and the next night, and no plane came up from Guadalcanal for him and the boy.

"There used to be some pigs on this island," the boy said. "If we could catch a pig. . . ." His eyes began to shine.

"You know how to cook a pig?" John asked him.

"No. But we've got a stove. Now if we had a pig. . . ."

"Okay, buddy. I catch, you cook." John got the gun and the knife. "You stay here and get ready to cook. I'll go get a pig."

"You'll have to shoot him," the boy said. "They can run faster than a wallaby."

"A what?"

"Don't you know what a wallaby is?"

"No, but if I catch one we'll eat him, too," John said, going out.

John wandered for an hour without seeing anything to eat except the impossible birds. No pigs. Anyway, he thought, if they can run so fast how would he get a pig even if he saw one?

But then the clouds began to form, big ones with wide, black, ominous bottoms and sparkling castled summits—and lumbered toward him. Within an hour the thunder was growling and shaking the ground, and lightning in spectacular bolts was hammering the mountainsides of Choiseul. Good pigging weather, John thought, working his way through the jungle looking for any signs of rooting.

He found them down under the coconut palms and so, picking himself out a spot where he could see the farthest through the grove, he sat down with his back against a tree, took out the pistol and waited. A little cooperation and co-ordination between that pig and Mother Nature and. . . .

Mother Nature came in first with a bang. He had never seen such a display of lightning nor heard thunder so close and hard. And *rain!* As he got colder and colder, he thought about the little house and wondered if the pig was worth it—especially since there was no sign of it.

And then there it was. It was standing in the rain about ten feet away from him and looking at him with a mean expression. It came one step closer and then turned and ran back out of sight.

John crept through the mud to another tree and sat down again. Soon the little pig reappeared and looked all around for him, still with that mean expression.

John settled the front sight down into the notch of the rear sight, and then set the little pig's left eye right on top of the square front sight. Now, he thought, is the time for Mother Nature.

But there was a lull in the uproar, and as the pig stood there, there wasn't a sound except the noise of the rain.

John was so hungry he started to shoot the pig anyway, hoping that a pistol shot would sound like thunder or something, but it didn't.

The pig stood there with that insulting ha-ha look on his face.

"Ha ha," John said aloud, and shifted the front sight so that it rested right between the pig's mean little eyes.

Then lightning crackled down and thunder came right behind it.

With all that noise even John didn't hear the gun. Nor did the pig.

As he picked it up, he said, "You're making a contribution to a worthy cause, friend."

They made a mess of things cooking that pig and it didn't taste very good when they ate it, but they agreed it was better than coconuts.

As they waited for nightfall, the boy explained a lot of things John had been wondering about.

Michael's father had been an overseer for the Lever Brothers Company, running the coconut plantations in these islands. It had been a good life, Michael said. He had had his own outrigger, and the school he had gone to hadn't taken up *too* much time. Once he had sailed with another kid all the way from Tulagi across to Guadalcanal. (John didn't tell him that this was now Iron Bottom Bay—the graveyard of many ships and many men.)

The war had wrecked everything, Michael told him. It was a good thing that when the war started, his mother had just left for a visit to Australia—she wouldn't have liked the way the Japanese acted.

He and his father had had to run for it, skipping from island to island in the night, hiding in the jungle, walking over mountains when they had to; stealing an outrigger when they could.

The tall man, Yamasaki, had been their real enemy, tracking them down no matter where they went. Yamasaki had once worked for his father, Michael said, but his father had caught him stealing and had beat him up. He should, Michael declared, have killed him then the way he wanted to.

His father, Michael said, had never run *away* from the

enemy. When they got too close he would move, but he never ran, never tried to escape to Australia. But he had tried to make Michael run away; but something always happened so he never could.

His father had joined the coastwatchers early, and from then on, they had taken the old 3B in the tin boxes with them wherever they had to go.

Finally though, Michael said, his father and he had sort of reached the end of the line. The Japs had moved in everywhere and there was no place left but this little island. But even here, Yamasaki had showed up.

That had been a bad time, and he had argued with his father about it. But his father had found a native he could trust, a man named Tingalap, and had sent Michael away in an outrigger.

They almost got away, too. But someone—a native or a Jap—had seen them and soon Yamasaki caught them. He had killed Tingalap and had tried to make Michael tell him where his father was hiding.

"I told him my father was dead," Michael said, "but I don't think he believed it because he kept on hurting me."

It had grown dark in the little house as Michael talked. John could barely see the boy sitting on the old cot.

"Then when they came with that gun, Yamasaki brought me down out of the hills. He said maybe *he* couldn't make me tell, but that they had ways to make me. That's why I ran that day. By that time I didn't much care what happened to me, Mr. Lawrence."

"My name is John," John said.

"But you're older than I am."

"Perhaps, but it's still John."

"Then when I was in the water, I thought they'd stop shooting at me if I seemed to be dead." The boy stopped talking and suddenly laughed. "I felt a little dead anyway."

"I know."

"Then when you came in the door that night, I saw you weren't my father so I thought . . . well. You see, I didn't know it was you."

"I'm glad you were a little weak. You're a good man with a knife."

They sat in the dark and didn't say anything for a while. Then the boy said, "What's going to happen . . . John?"

"We'll be all right. The Marines know where we are. They'll take care of us."

"If they'll drop us some food, we can stay and spy on the Japs until they lose the war."

"Let's talk to them about that right now," John said, switching on the 3B and watching the tubes begin to glow. In a little while he called Guadalcanal again, reported the weather and assured the corporal (he wondered what had happened to the other voice—the dry, skeptical and derisive one) that it would be perfectly safe now to make an airdrop on you-know-who island.

That was one of the things that bothered the corporal. Those code names—Clementine and Peggy Ann and all the rest—were about as top secret as you could get. If that guy, on Clementine was a Jap, how did he know the code name? And if the Japs knew top secret stuff like that, then something ought to be done. But the corporal was sick and the major was sick, so the corporal told himself that after this chill that was racking him out passed, he was going to do something about it.

He didn't, because after the chill passed a fever hit him. It was so hot he felt like taking his skin off.

So John and the boy waited through another long night and only the bombers, droning and then hissing over him

and droning away, came to his island. He climbed down
and reported them and the Wildcats were up there again waiting.

In the operations tent at Henderson Field no one wondered much about where the dope on the bombers was coming from or whether the man who was sending it was a spy
for the enemy or not. It was good dope and the Wildcat
pilots were having a turkey shoot up there, and the bombs
weren't coming down on them the way they had. So—who
cared?

And another night passed and another. John and the boy
ate the last of the pig and went back to coconuts and roots,
for John never found another pig on that island.

He couldn't understand why the plane never came from
Guadalcanal or if they couldn't spare one, why the *Enterprise* didn't let one of its regular search planes drop him
some food. If they just took the scraps from the galley. . . .

At last the corporal couldn't understand it either, and he
was getting so that he couldn't stand to hear radio X's pleas
for food—for help. Nothing went past Clementine without
radio X letting them know, so why, the corporal asked only
himself, couldn't they help the poor guy?

And then one day a buddy of his from radio Tulagi drifted
in through the mud, and the corporal talked to him about it.
His buddy was a man of influence (to hear him tell it) and
claimed to be a personal friend of President Roosevelt's and
although the officers *thought* they ran the Skimmer outfit,
actually his old buddy was the brains behind it all. Don't
worry, he'd take care of everything. He knew the lieutenant
personally and kept him in line.

The corporal watched his buddy drift away through the
rain and decided that nothing would come of that, but at
least somebody had agreed with him that something ought

to be done about the guy running radio X. The fact that his buddy was only a radioman third class, and would probably be busted within the week, forced the corporal to doubt that he was going to take over from Nimitz and end this war by Thursday.

10

This is the night to drop that food, John thought, as he wearily climbed up the little steps cut into the tree and settled down on his platform.

Perhaps, he thought and hoped, this is the night they've been waiting for—the full moon, no rain, a gentle westerly wind so that the drop wouldn't be blown out to sea.

A perfect night for it and he searched the sky and listened hard and *hoped*.

A little cloud that must have been left over from something drifted over him and on toward Choiseul with nothing particular to do.

And again the sound tricked him for he had been waiting —night after night after night—for the sound of a single plane from the south.

This sound came from the sea and was the slow, low throbbing of a ship.

The sea, in the glasses, was a solid, sparkling silver in the moonlight so that the little freighter looked very black and sharply outlined. If it was not the same one which had brought the gun, it was one exactly like it.

When the ship turned ninety degrees at the end of his island, John realized that he had known it would. And now in a moment it would make another ninety-degree turn and then come to anchor just beyond the native village.

The ship did just that, and John sat and watched the loading booms swing outboard, lifting the barge up and lowering it into the water.

Because he didn't want to think about it, it took a long time for him to admit that this was total disaster. As soon as men from that ship got ashore and found the slaughter the grenades had made, they were going to come looking for him.

He sat there watching them unloading crates and bales onto the barge and he could hear them yelling and knew that they were yelling to the men who no longer existed on the shore. It wouldn't be long now.

John gathered up his little accumulation of belongings—the glasses, the box of ammo for the pistol, the Marine dagger, the signaling mirror—and climbed down out of the tree.

He woke up Michael and told him about the ship in the channel as he lit the Coleman and began disconnecting the radio, putting each unit of it into the metal boxes. The boy went around the little house erasing all signs of their having been in it as John went out and in the moonlight dug a trench, buried the radio, covered it and scattered leaves and branches over the raw scar.

He knew in his heart that there was no need to climb the tree again; knew exactly what he would see.

They were coming. The ship's boat, full of them, was towing the barge, which was packed with more of them, straight across the channel toward his island. On shore he could see their dark figures searching cautiously through the jungle.

Moonlight glinted off their rifle barrels and little round helmets as they came closer and closer.

John stood on the platform for a moment longer, watching

them. At least, he thought, I am not going to be confused by having to make a choice from among many things.

As he climbed down the tree he thought about the boy. His mind searched for other ways, other escapes for that boy, but finally gave up. There was only one way to go. It was not an escape, John knew. It was only prevention.

Michael was waiting in the house. "They're on the island," John told him, getting out the Mae West and sticking the stuff back into the loops and pockets. "They'll be up here soon."

"What are we going to do?" the boy asked.

John started to tell him and then thought: What right have I to tell this boy anything? He isn't my brother, nor my son. He belongs to someone else, someone I don't even know.

"You can come with me," John said. "If you want to."

"I want to," the boy said.

"I don't think. . . ." John stopped and looked at him. Why tell him? John thought. What good does it do to tell him that we're going out there and swim until we stop swimming? What good?

The boy didn't say anything. He just held out his hand. In it were the thick silver dog tags on the heavy chain which John's mother had given him because she hadn't liked the thin aluminum ones the Navy had issued him. "Thanks," John said, hanging them around his neck.

He put the Mae West on the boy and tied it tight around him, then he showed him how to blow it up with the tubes.

"Let's go," he said.

They left the shack and keeping in the shadows, started for the path.

They had circled the covered pit fall and were going down the path when John suddenly remembered the diary.

"Be right back," he said. "Wait."

He turned and ran back to the house and got the little moldy book and ran back out of the house.

The man saw him at the same instant John saw the man. He was wearing a helmet and a greenish uniform and carrying a flimsy looking, thin-barreled rifle.

John fired at him with the pistol and ran, skirting the pit fall.

He had missed with the pistol. The man was coming full blast past the house. . . .

To the boy standing in the shadows, John whispered, "Run!" and he went ahead of him down the path, running fast on bare feet.

John turned and saw the man coming. And then saw him disappear instantly and then heard him scream as the stakes at the bottom of the pit got him.

John turned and followed the boy.

They were careful going through the open areas under the palms, but on the beach with no protection at all they simply ran for the sea.

John never even saw the soldier standing in the water. He didn't see the muzzle flash or hear the rifle crack.

One minute he was running beside the boy. Then something with the weight of a freight train hit him and knocked him backwards—he could feel his heels sliding backwards in the hard sand. Then he was lying on his back.

The man was firing at Michael who was splashing through the water, throwing up sheets of silvery water.

John felt no real pain, just a great, heavy numbness as he turned on one side and shot the man, watching him drop the rifle, spin around and fall, rolling down so that the little waves lapped against him.

Michael came back then and helped him crawl down to

the sea and into it. Then he swam straight away from the island, pulling John with him for now pain was starting, and he discovered that he could not move his arms at all.

Bullets were coming from the beach. He could hear the little, sad whine they made and the hard, dry smack when they hit the water. Looking back, the whole beach seemed to be lined with men, the rifle muzzles flashing dimly like tired fireflies. In a little while an angry machine gun started up, and the bullets around them sounded like clapping from dry, hard hands.

Michael swam steadily, one arm around his waist. At each stroke he made a wave which rolled over his shoulder and struck John in the face, and he concentrated then on not breathing when the wave came over.

The shooting stopped with a suddenness which, because it had no reason, alarmed him.

Then he saw the man swimming toward him. His arms were flailing away, shattering the silvery water and he was coming very fast, a plume of water rising around his heels.

"One's in the water," he said to the boy.

Michael stopped swimming and turned his head.

Then he turned John loose, his arm sliding away from him. As John sank he felt hands touching him here and there, but he was too concerned with getting his face above water again to think about it.

When he could see again, he found that the man had stopped a few feet away from him and was treading water, looking at him. The man's head was perfectly round and shaved clean so that in the moonlight it looked like metal. John could hear his breathing as now his arm and hand appeared above the water.

John saw the pistol then and watched as the man with a

curious deliberateness shook the water out of the barrel before pointing it at him.

Without his arms to pull him John could not go down into the sea. He tried but could not.

The man made a low, grunting sound and slowly lowered his arm, the pistol going out of sight below the silvery water.

Something in the sea grabbed John and jerked him below the surface so violently that he could not even draw in his breath. As he struggled to get his legs free of it, he was dragged through the water, deeper and deeper.

Then it shoved him up again, so that he could breathe.

The man seemed very far away, lying face down in the water.

Michael appeared beside John, put his arm around him and began to swim again.

His island suddenly seemed far away now. Just a white, gleaming line of beach with the dark jungle behind it.

John turned his head and looked out across The Slot.

A million miles of empty sea, silver in the moonlight.

11

"Radio X," the corporal said wearily, "This is Guadalcanal. Come in, Come in."

There was no answer.

He looked at the clock and waited and flipped the switch again. "Radio X. Come in, please. I have a message for you."

No answer.

He waited and watched the clock and wondered how the major was getting along. They had finally come for him and carried him away; just a thing of yellow skin and bones that looked like they would break through it and a little, whispery voice protesting all the way. "I'm all right," the major kept whispering to them as they rolled him in the blanket and carried him away. "Let me alone, I'm all right!"

Then the Australian came in, wearing that crazy hat.

"'Ow's it, Corporal?" the Aussie asked, sucking on a cigar about the size of a pencil and at least a foot long now that it was half-smoked. And it was bent in the middle.

"No answer," the corporal said, thinking that this Australian's skin would make a good saddle for a horse. Just the right toughness.

"Probably the IF can. Always potting out on the 3Bs. I'll go up tomorrow and relieve the poor bloke and have it fixed in a jiffy."

"You do that," the corporal said, turning back to the transmitter. "Radio X. Come in. Come in. I have a steak on a sizzling platter for you."

There was nothing but a hum from the speaker.

"Hope nothing's gone wrong up there," the Australian said, looking at his cigar.

"You can have that sitting in the bushes by yourself with them sneaking up on you. I'll take Guadalcanal or even Mott Street," the corporal said, thinking that it took a *man* to smoke a cigar that smelled as bad as this one.

"Hope they haven't sneaked up on him and buggered the set," the Australian said.

"What about *him?*" the corporal asked indignantly, not knowing and not caring what the things on the Australian's shirt stood for (as long as he wasn't a Marine). "Maybe he's got a knife in his back or a bullet through his head or they've strung him up by his. . . .

There was a voice coming from the speaker and he whirled around. But it was the SW from Tulagi.

"Okay, ol' buddy," the voice said, "I just talked to Franklin D. and all is copacetic."

Holy crow!, the corporal thought, those Navy swabbies get away with saying *anything* over the air.

"Stop beating your toothless gums," the corporal said into the microphone, "I'm trying to listen to the radio."

12

Michael had stopped swimming and turned John loose. He had the tube from the throat of the Mae West in his mouth and was blowing into it steadily.

The thing wasn't inflating and when John noticed bubbles coming up, he told him to feel around and see if it had a hole in it.

It did have. A bullet had slit it open across the back.

"It won't do you any good then, so take if off," John told him.

Michael untied it and wriggled his arms out of it. John watched the yellow thing floating away as the boy put his arm back around him and started swimming again.

John was beginning to know now that he was terribly hurt and could not long survive. Unable to touch where the bullet had hit him, he could not tell exactly what damage it had done. But he could barely breathe, and each inhalation was becoming more difficult.

"Don't swim," he told Michael.

Treading water, the boy held him up. "Is it bad?" he asked.

"Yeah, it is. Pretty bad."

He was trying to think, but thoughts were like little clouds drifting in and out of his mind. He couldn't catch them and hold them.

But one came in then and stayed for a little while. "You'd better go back to Choiseul. Hide in the jungle. They won't stay long."

He wondered for a second why the boy didn't say anything, but that got lost too. A little cloud drifting on about its business.

It got very quiet and peaceful there. Michael, he guessed, must have left him because he couldn't feel the arm around him any more and nothing was moving.

It was funny, he thought. This must be just about where Jeff's plane, blazing in that long-ago night, must have struck the sea and gone down. He thought about Jeff and his mother and father and was glad that it was so quiet here and warm and still, with nothing else to think about at all.

He didn't hear the sound, nor see the dark hull, nor hear the mop-headed man with the Harvard accent say, "Hold your fire. It's only a boy."

And another, incredulous voice say, "Only a *what!*"

John didn't feel the surge of the Packard engines just under him as the PT boat swung around the south end of his island, fired one torpedo into the freighter and spun in a great mass of silver spray and was gone for Guadalcanal, three-quarters of the long, shining black hull clear of the sea, the Packards drumming and the long, V'd wake dying out behind it.

John felt no one lift him and carry him below decks where there was light. The lean lieutenant, his mop of hair plastered down by spray, came in and looked down at him as the corpsman gently cut away the flight suit from around the smashed zipper.

They looked at John's chest where the bullet had hit him

and the lieutenant said in awe, "Look what it did to those dog tags!"

The corpsman touched John gently with his fingers. "Just broke his breast bone, I think." Then he turned his face up to the lieutenant. "How lucky can you get?"

"Yeah," the lieutenant said.

"Maybe some ribs, too. But this one'll live to fight another day."

"How's the kid?" the lieutenant asked.

"Okay. He's got an old bullet wound—right through him. But he says it doesn't hurt any more." He looked up at the lieutenant. "Hope my kids turn out like that one."

"They will," the lieutenant said, going topside again.

13

The nurse paid the girl behind the counter in the hospital PX, told her never mind wrapping the little box and went out into the sunshine.

It was a beautiful day in Hawaii. As the nurse walked along, she opened the box and looked at the shiny gold wings lying in the purple velvet. He'd like this, she thought.

She had finally learned to look at them when they brought them in from the ships without crying, but when they had brought him in she couldn't help it. She *knew* him. She had nursed him before and to see him coming back to her had just been too much.

Now he was lying on his back on the grass, his arms under his head, and looking up at the travel poster sky. She shut the little box and patted the pocket of her starched uniform to be sure it was there and walked over to him.

She had finally learned, too, that no matter how badly

they were hurt (and some of them were ruined), they wanted to go back so there was no use any more wondering about it.

"Hi, John," she said. "Here's a present for you." She dropped the box on his stomach. She hadn't meant to do it this way, but this is the way she did it.

He strained his head up, looked at the box, took one hand from under his head, opened the box, looked at the wings before they fell out on his chest and then looked up at her.

"What are you trying to do, Nell? Make me look like I just came out from Stateside?"

"I know all about you Navy types," she said. "You soak your gold braid in sea water and tarnish your wings so you'll look salty. I'm not impressed."

"Vicissitudes of war," he said. He fumbled for the wings with his fingers. "Thanks, Nell."

"Warriors," she said.

As soon as she gave him the orders, it would be the end of him—as far as she was concerned. The end.

Unless, she thought and then put it far away, he comes back to me again from some other desolate place, hurt again, perhaps this time finally destroyed.

She took the letter out of her pocket and dropped that, too, on his chest.

He squinted against the brilliant sunlight, skipped the From To Via and read the Subject. Then he sat up, furious.

"*Pensacola!*" he yelled. "They can't send me to Pensacola. I don't want to go to Pensacola."

"Read the rest of it," she said.

She watched him and knew exactly when he got to the words. She saw him close his eyes slowly and then open them and say out loud but, she knew, only to himself, "'Report for duty involving flying.'"

"How about that?" he said, whispering. "How *about* that?"

He raised his arm, moving it around. Then he picked up the gold wings again and looked at them.

Then he looked up at her.

It's time to go, she thought. He's a naval aviator again and so forever lost to her.

As she turned away from him, she saw that Australian kid, Michael, walking with his mother across the grass. Coming to say good-by to John Lawrence.

The nurse suddenly turned back for a moment and said, "Don't get hurt any more, John."

"All right," he said. Then he saw the boy coming. He put the wings back in the box. "Do you mind if I give them to him?" he asked the nurse.

"No," she said, "I don't mind."